I0615059

H.E.R.S.T.O.R.Y

Happiness Is Possible, Just You Wait and See!

by

CARLOTTA ANE'TH

Andrea Johnson Books Publishing

H.E.R.S.T.O.R.Y

© 2020 CarlottaAne'th. All rights reserved

Cover art designed by Andrea Johnson.

No part of this book may be reproduced, stored in a retrieval system, or transmitted by any means without the written permission of the author.

First published by Andrea Johnson Books Publishing.
10/20/2020
6565 N. MacArthur Blvd, Suite 225 Dallas, TX. 75039
www.Ajbpublishing.com

This is a work of fiction. Names, characters, places and incidents either are a product of the author's imagination, or used fictitiously. Any resemblance to actual persons, living or dead, events or locales, is entirely coincidental.

Because of the dynamic nature of the Internet, any web addresses or links contained in this book may have changed since publication and may no longer be valid. The views expressed in this work are solely those of the author and do not necessarily reflect the views of the publisher, and the publisher herby disclaims any responsibility for them.

ISBN: 978-0-578-78244-7

Dedication

H.E.R.S.T.O.R.Y. is dedicated first to my Queen Mother Jewell Dell aka 'The Bird'. Her life I most definitely did not understand when I was a child. The events in her life she endured for my King brothers Ahmad aka 'Red' and Sweeney aka 'Ric Brenin' and myself as a young girl and woman I thought I would never understand. I soon came to understand completely and could relate to H.E.R.S.T.O.R.Y. which soon became mine, only I chose to break the curse forever.

With that being said I also dedicate this book and story to my children Clarissa aka 'thekitchenbruja', Crysta aka 'Charley', Caryna aka 'Beauty', Chania aka 'Nana', Ciara aka 'Princess', Michael aka 'Junior', and Malachi aka 'Poppas'. I could never have written this book without their encouragement and LOVE they showered on me and their very presence in my life's journey. I am the woman/Queen I am today because of them.
To my Grandchildren the love I have for them I cannot explain Keira, Onias, Cameron, Olivia and Jace new chapters in my life.

To the two women/Queens who were ever present no matter where I lived who helped to mold me into the woman/Queen I am, Linda Williams my beloved Sister and my BFF whom I call Sister God-mother to all my children who made herself ever present in their lives and mine. No one will ever understand or know the love I have for her, but her and Abba Stephanie Ann Pride-Jones aka 'Auntie Nephanie'

To the Great I am, my Abba Father true King in my life, thank you for "Never leaving Nor forsaking me" You are my source, my strength, my first, my last and the beginning and the end. I love You more than words can say!

"One last love to share, to my King he knows who he is" I love you JM!

And to all the Women/Queens who have endured the hardship of being a mother, a wife and friend may your story be told via H.E.R.S.T.O.R.Y.

- CarlottaAne'th

Foreword

I've never met a more valiant or more beautiful spirit, such as

CarlottaAne'th. Her journey and testimony are one of the most heart

gripping stories you will ever hear. And not simply because of the events

in which she recaptures with such clarity. But because of her unshakeable

perseverance to ensure that her voice was heard. As you read on, you will

become a part of, H.E.R.S.T.O.R.Y As CarlottaAne'th draws you in with

each memory, and the carefully crafted characters that showcase the

message in detail.

Her words give an emotionally powerful reality, to the very dark truth

that is still existing among women and girls today. There is no way you

will not be moved by her rendition of thoughts and creativity.

I am honored to know someone such as CarlottaAne'th. She has taken

what is a monumentally challenging issue, and turned it into a positive

resource for women today. At least eight out of ten women in America

have been abused sexually, psychologically, emotionally and mentally.

And many find it hard to voice the pain that has no name, and a shame

that has no ending. But with CarlottaAne'th's words and courage, she has made it possible for women and young girls everywhere to realize their worth. To find their strength. And to speak their voice. She has touched me immensely with her astounding faith and resilience. And I am certain that her words will help many others who are searching to find and give power to their own story....by witnessing hers.

-   *Andrea Johnson*

H.E.R.S.T.O.R.Y

Prologue

Nichelle Turner, a strong black American born woman, highly educated and Child Psychologist enamored with her life as a mother, was seeking the one thing she desired most, a love of her own here on Earth. A love she never truly received or felt as a little girl, only to find herself in deep dark despair of hate and violence.

Nichelle never thought her happiness was possible. She doubted any love outside of God, even though she gave her heart to him, but truly desired an earthly relationship. She thought she'd found it in her ex-husband Mark Sr. But Nichelle then met Roger, the man she assumed would also be that commitment she longed for. She'd truly believed happiness was now possible, only to find that he was a horrible life-threatening mistake that left her second guessing everything in her life. Thereafter, it had all come into question. Including the very love God did send her, Frank Martin.

Just You Wait and See, What Comes Next...

Chapter 1

"Oh my goodness," Nichelle said to herself, as she looked at the clock on the wall realizing she was running late.

"I'm late! I hope he understands...even after what I have to tell him."

Nichelle took a second look at her attire, peering into her favorite mirror leaning up against the wall of her master-bedroom, her most prized possession. A gift she received from her ex-husband Mark Sr., before they divorced. The mirror stood almost 7 feet tall, trimmed with beautiful white oak carvings, which matched perfectly and accentuated the wood trim in her bedroom along the ceiling walls.

She stood in front of it turning several times to assure she chose the right outfit held in her hands.

She felt it was perfect. Nichelle then decided to adorn herself with the pair of white jeans that fit her voluptuous full-figured body, along with a yellow blouse she felt made her look old. Believing that the outfit would lessen her appeal as the woman he desired.

But after trying it on, Nichelle didn't like the white espadrilles she was wearing. So she walked back into the closet and pulled out a pair of white and yellow colored Toms.

"Now I am ready." she muttered, as she headed for the bedroom door, only to be startled by her son Christopher.

"Momma, where are you going?" Christopher asked with curiosity.

"I have a date, son; I'll see you later this evening. I promise I'll be back before you go to sleep." Nichelle said quickly.

"Okay Mom." Christopher gave a little smirk, as he kissed her forehead, towering over her, standing at 6 ft tall. "Boy, you need to stop growing." She chuckled, shaking her head as she walked down the stairs and out the door to her jalopy of a car. Suddenly a quick thought came into her head, "one day, I'll have the car I desire." She nodded her head to encourage herself, while making her way to the car.

Nichelle left her house by way of the kitchen through the garage door. She stepped down into the outer level, but not before hitting the switch to open the doors.

Getting into her car, she started up her jalopy, shaking her head from the sounds it was making.

Rolling down the driveway, she hit the button for the garage door and began thinking to herself, lost in thought.

'How did I let this get so far past me, what do I say? How will I tell him without bringing bitterness between us?'

Nichelle began to muddle over her thoughts, her mind wandering back to the first time she met Frank Martin, and the events that followed.

***

It was an appointment she'd attended for a mutual client between Frank, his team, and herself. During the meeting they'd discussed the concerns of the client and what their needs were, and how to make the treatment plan successful for them. But while they were talking, a strange thing began to happen.

During the conversation, after all the introductions with Frank's team, Nichelle's heart began to beat really fast, her palms became moist, and she was sweating profusely. She didn't feel so good.

'Oh my god' she thought to herself, 'I'm having a panic attack! Please not here, not now, they'll think I'm unprofessional. I'll lose the client and the backing!'

The last time she'd had a panic attack like this, was when she was with Roger.

Meanwhile, Frank was staring at Nichelle from across the table watching her every move. He was first and foremost mesmerized by her beauty, her caramel bronze skin intrigued him. Thinking to himself, Frank's emotions were in a turmoil.

'Oh my god, she is absolutely beautiful. All that bubbling brown sugar sitting over there.' Frank could not stop staring at her. His thoughts wandered, and he began to fantasize at what she smelled like; how soft her hands would be in his. But he made an effort to reign in his wayward thoughts.

"No Frank." Shaking his head subtly so no one noticed, he whispered to himself. "Stay focused."

He began to pray silently under his breath.

Nichelle finally composed herself, 'get it together girl' she berated herself in her mind. She grabbed a napkin from her bag and patted her forehead.

Suddenly Frank reached over, he touched her hand and formed the words silently, asking her, "are you okay?"

He felt something when he touched her, a tingling from her hand to his. He leaned back in his seat after she nodded and responded silently, "I'm okay."

He rubbed his hand as if it were sore to the touch. Frank began to feel somewhat ashamed because of the thoughts he was having for her.

Nichelle started to feel the tension, and thought to herself, 'should I leave?' but she didn't want to interrupt the person speaking. Thinking it would appear rude. So she concentrated on hearing what the client's needs were, and how she could implement them, all while feeling like running out of the room.

Chapter 2

Her thoughts were off, and she could barely concentrate, but managed to make it through the first meeting. When the conversation was done, they scheduled for several more meetings to have concrete findings for the client's final evaluation.

Nichelle quickly pulled her thoughts in for the time being. She feared any further contact would send her in a whirlwind of emotions. So as soon as the conference was over, she began to pack up her laptop and the rest of her things, and hurriedly made her way to the door, hoping not to have any interaction with Frank outside of business. There was something about him in particular that rattled her senses.

But as soon as she grabbed for the doorknob to leave, he was there. Standing next to her, he said casually, "good night Mrs. Turner, looking forward to seeing you at the next meeting."

Nichelle didn't correct him from calling her 'Mrs.' instead she simply nodded her head, and walked out to her car.

Nichelle was flustered, her cheeks felt warm, even hot to the touch. She had to take several breathes so she could drive home. 'This is crazy, I am completely out of sorts.' she thought to herself.

Frank watched in awe of her as she departed, her smell captured him, everything about her intrigued him, and he wanted to know more.

Simultaneously, Nichelle walked to her car and began to think how amazing Frank had smelled. He was so handsome and sexy, his skin was like milk chocolate, she felt a tingle when he'd touched her hand, and it felt good.

"Oh no" Nichelle said to herself, she shook her head, trying to bring her thoughts in. She started her car and headed home.

Frank promised himself, that at the next meeting he would introduce himself properly. He couldn't get her out of his head, her beauty, her lips. How her hand tingled in his. He'd felt something when he touched her. 'I need more of her.' He thought.

Upon entering her car and driving, Nichelle began to breathe deeply, as her therapist taught her in a crisis. She called her Sister Naomi while sitting in her car, to tell her what was happening. But she'd also called because she sensed something was going on with Naomi as well.

Naomi picked up and answered, and Nichelle just began to talk in a rush of words.

"Naomi, what do I do? This guy is flustering me!" "Excuse me Sis, Hello and, how are you?" Naomi laughed and responded to her sister's banter with humor.

"Oh, Naomi I am sorry, I'm having a panic attack. Please help me. Ever since I've been in this guy's presence; I've been having a melt down!" Nichelle's voice had a slight tremble to it, as she explained.

Naomi started to laugh. "Why are you laughing, Sis?" Nichelle said, annoyed. Naomi replied, "Nichelle, remember how you felt when you met Mark?"

Mark was the father of Nichelle's children and ex-husband. "Remember Sis, that's when you first started having panic attacks."

"Oh my god." Nichelle said in shock. "What do I do now? I can't have this happen."

The panic started to rise as Nichelle's thoughts raced.

"Naomi, I do remember now, and I married Mark two years thereafter, this cannot happen!"

Naomi could not stop laughing at her sister.

"Stop laughing, this isn't funny!" Nichelle complained, and Naomi began to encourage her, but it was not really working.

"Use your techniques Nichelle, don't let it get to you." Naomi tried give her some reassurance.

Nichelle replied halfheartedly that she would, and said goodbye, but then Naomi interrupted her.

"Wait, Nichelle I need to tell you something. Do you have a few moments?"

"Of course, what's up?"

"Tristan is having an affair" Naomi's voice trailed off as the words left her mouth.

"What?! No he loves you, he would never." Nichelle responded quickly.

"Yes, he did!" Naomi shot the words out in bitterness.

The phone line was silent until Nichelle asked, "How long has this been going on?"

"He has been seeing her for a year." Naomi tells her.

"Oh no Naomi, I am sorry. What are you going to do? Will you file for a divorce? What do you plan to do?"

"Nichelle, it's not that simple."

"What do you mean...?"

Naomi interrupts and says, "Nichelle, she is pregnant. the baby is Tristan's."

Nichelle shakes her head in sadness. "Naomi, yes it is simple. Divorce him, let her have him."

As Naomi pushed away the lump in her throat and tears started to roll down her face she said, "Nichelle, she is married too."

"Okay, To who?" Nichelle asked her.

"Bishop!"

"Bishop who?"

"Bishop Sanchez"

"What?!" Nichelle exclaimed in surprise. She parked and turned the engine to her car off and sat in silence, speechless.

Naomi continued to tell Nichelle the whole story and how Tristan wanted to take care of the baby, but Marie, the woman he was seeing, refuses to cooperate.

"She is too terrified to tell Bishop and has already shared with him that she is with child."

Nichelle couldn't believe it. "But they announced her pregnancy at service months ago!" She said to her sister in amazement. "Naomi, this is not good, now what?"

"Tristan is going to convince her to tell Bishop or he will." Naomi said quietly.

"This is awkward!" Nichelle said in frustration.

"I know. But please do not say anything." Naomi asked her, her voice sounding strained.

"I won't. But Naomi this is going to be ugly. I will be praying."

24

"Okay, Nichelle I must go Tristan is coming in, talk to you later."

"This conversation is not over. I will call you soon and you keep me updated." Nichelle said with resolve.

"Will do, love you Sis" Naomi replied.

"Love you too."

Nichelle sat in silence, not sure what to say about the whole conversation. Suddenly her panic attack didn't seem so important. She started the car up again, and headed home.

Chapter 3

Nichelle finally arrived home, and the house seemed empty and quiet, but she knew everyone was asleep. She looked in on the children and then headed to the kitchen. Walking across the large space to her pantry, she slowly opened the door as to not wake the children and grabbed a bottle of Cabernet from her wine rack. She came out of the pantry and grabbed a glass as well, heading for her room and closing the door behind her.

Nichelle slowly opened the bottle of wine with ease, pulling the cork out, for it had already been opened. She pondered on the events of the day. As she poured the wine, filling the glass almost to the top, she took a sip while replaying the whole scenario with Roger in her mind. Her dark thoughts taking her back to the man who had left her with many regrets.

She pushed off her shoes and stepped up into her bed by way of her step stool, also a gift from her ex-husband and children, for her birthday. She didn't even bother to remove her clothing, just laid across the bed where she fell fast asleep.

She drifted into a deep slumber. When she woke up all her clothes were off and she had a night gown on, and she was under the covers.

'I don't remember taking my clothes off.'

Nichelle thought with confusion, but began to stir in her bed to get ready for the day. She prepared herself to take a shower as she always did, carefully picking and selecting her attire for the day. She was meticulous with what she planned to wear, from the earrings to her shoes.

She got dressed and applied her make-up and headed downstairs for coffee, while running into the children, and grabbing her green goodness smoothie from the fridge. She said her good mornings and goodbyes to the children for the day.

But just as she was headed to the garage, Mark Jr stopped her by the door.

"Momma did you leave the garage door open after you came in?" He asked her abruptly.

Nichelle frowned in dismay as she looked at him.

"No son, I didn't leave the garage door open. I always close it after I pull in."

"Well, the garage door was open all night, mom. When I took the garbage out to the curb this morning, it was open. I asked Chris, but he was sleeping and didn't even know what I was saying to him."

"Jr are you sure!" Nichelle questioned him.

"Yes, I'm positive."

Nichelle shook her head in befuddlement and thought maybe she did forget, but suddenly realized she was running late and ran out the door.

Arriving for her meeting, Nichelle apologized for her lateness and the team immediately began the proceedings by reviewing the evaluations.

Just as they were finishing up, Frank walked over to Nichelle to introduce himself properly this time. He extended his hand to her and said, "Hi, I'm Frank Martin."

She grabbed it reluctantly and he shook her hand ever so gently. Nichelle thought she would scream out loud, but her screams and anguish were in her head, reeling from his touch.

She felt herself inwardly swooning and quickly pulled her hand back.

"Hi, I'm Nichelle Turner." she replied in a curt voice, so as not to show her true feelings.

And it was from that encounter Frank began to pursue Nichelle. He knew he had to have her, and believed she was meant to be his wife someday.

Frank began his pursuit, and Nichelle continued to run from him after every meeting, knowing he wanted to talk to her, so she would quickly escape.

One evening, Nichelle was sitting in her den watching a movie with her twin girls, but actually the movie was watching them.

The girls were fast asleep in her lap when her cell phone began to vibrate, moving on the coffee table. She jumped up to grab for the phone as it started to fall onto the floor. She tried to catch it before hitting the ground, careful not to wake the girls. Nichelle grabbed the phone in her hands and slowly proceeded to answer.

As she did so, she saw Frank's name and hesitated, but her thumb ran over the answer button by accident, and she immediately felt regret.

Nichelle placed the phone to her ear in slow motion, feeling trepidation, but heard his voice clearly.

"Hello, may I speak to Nichelle?"

She didn't want to answer. His voice did something to her, it made her melt from the inside out. She was flustered. After an awkward silence, she finally responded.

"Good evening, this is Nichelle."

She was unaware of it, but to Frank her voice was bubbly, and it absolutely drove him crazy.

"Hi, this is Frank Martin. How are you this evening?"

"Hi Frank, I'm doing well, how are you doing?"

Wanting to say why are you calling me, Nichelle chose to perform the polite banter instead.

Frank continued, "I'm doing better now that I finally made this call. I've been trying to reach you for the past two hours" he chuckled.

"Oh, I don't see that you called, there are no miscalls from you." Nichelle frowned, looking at her phone.

"Well, no you wouldn't see a miscall. I just called for the first time. I had cold feet ten times prior to this conversation. I finally dialed and let it ring." Frank was honest with her. That was refreshing.

"Oh," Nichelle chuckled and responded with a slight smile.

"Well, I would like to ask if you would join me for worship service this Sunday." Frank came out and asked her.

Nichelle paused briefly but then said, "sure, I would love... um I mean I would like to."

"Okay." Frank replied with a smile in his voice. "I look forward to seeing you this Sunday then. Have a good evening. Oh, and I'll be picking you up. I'll give you a call when I'm on my way."

"What time should I be ready?" Nichelle asked him. "I'll be by around 10am, so I'll see you then."

Frank needed to make the call short and quick for he was nervous that he would say something crazy, tell her how he wanted her in every way possible. His thoughts about Nichelle consumed him. He wanted her more than anything on earth.

"Have a nice evening Frank." Nichelle said softly.

You too Nichelle, Good night!"

He hung up immediately without hesitation. Thinking to himself how amazing it would be to watch her sleep, prepare dinner together and make love to her, taking her to a place neither of them has never been.

His thoughts were to make her feel like a Queen. He was smitten, and all he wanted was her.

Chapter 4

Nichelle went to sleep with Frank on her mind. She dreamed a dream so vivid and felt so real, that when she woke up, she saw her hand touching the empty side of the bed, reaching for someone who was not there... Frank.

Nichelle sat up in her bed sweating profusely and breathing like she was just in a marathon.

"Oh my goodness, I'm dreaming about this man now." Nichelle shook her head with her palm on her forehead, thinking to herself, 'what have I done? I've opened a can of worms.'

Sitting up in her bed, she looked at her clock that was positioned across the room on her dresser, that just happened to match her favorite mirror. Also a gift from her ex-husband, Mark Sr.

Nichelle realized it was time to get ready. But just then, she heard a knock at her bedroom door.

"Come in." She called out.

Christopher and Mark Jr. walked into the room, each yielding a little girl in their arms.

"Momma we've dressed the girls, how do they look?" Mark Jr. asked, pleased with himself.

"The girls are not happy, Mom" said Christopher. Dina had a look of pure disappointment and despair on her face.

"What's wrong beauty?" Nichelle asked Dina, taking her in her arms.

"Mommy I don't like these shoes Christopher put on me, they are not right." Dina complained, sulkily.

Nichelle called Dina beauty, because of how beautiful her dark skin was, it was always shining and very smooth.

"And you, little Miss?" she turned to her other daughter, Dana.

"Me too Momma, my shoes are all wrong. Mark and Christopher are terrible shoe pickers" Dana added.

Nichelle did everything she could to not laugh, she covered her mouth and chuckled at their protests. Smiling at her little Princess' Nichelle said, "Yes, they are baby girl, Mommy will fix it."

Nichelle examined the girls and made a quick switch of their shoes.

"Is this better my loves?"

In unison the girls chimed, "Yes Mommy!"

Mark Jr. spoke up, "Can we go now; I have a sound check in a couple of minutes, I'm late."

"Sure, you guys go on I'll see you later for dinner." Christopher grabbed the hands of Dana and Dina, but turned around as he was walking out the room, and asked, "Momma you going to church with Auntie Naomi?"

Nichelle raised her voice slightly and replied "No, I am not. I'm going with a friend; I'll see you guys later."

Shrugging his shoulders Christopher responded, "Okay, I was just wondering, sorry Momma."

"It's okay my love, I'm sorry for snapping. I love you, enjoy service and pray for me."

"I always do Momma."

They gave her a kiss on the forehead and the boys kissed her hand and headed out the door.

"Thank you, Christopher and Mark, for dressing the girls and I will see you for dinner, okay? I promise."

Nichelle said to them as they walked out.

"You are welcome Momma, we love you, later." Christopher replied, then left with the others.

She walked back into her bedroom to prepare herself. As Nichelle went into the bathroom to take a shower, she reached to turn on the water when she heard her phone ring.

She almost ran across the room to pick it up from her nightstand. Glancing at the phone and seeing Frank's name, she became excited, she felt her heart begin to race. Nichelle answered, trying to compose herself.

"Hello Frank!" she said, trying not to sound so excited to hear his voice.

"Good morning Nichelle, I must drop my boys off first and then I will be by to pick you up, is this alright?" Frank asked her.

"Yes, that's fine, I'm running a little slow this morning so no problem, I'll see you soon." Nichelle Replied to him, and gave him her address.

Knowing she had to settle her own children as well, she completely understood. Nichelle's thoughts began to flow around Frank. He was a Godly man, which seemed enough for her, but she still had reservations, a fear beneath it all. But instead, she kept going. She thought to herself, Roger supposedly loved God too, but not enough to worship with her. As she thought of her previous relationship, fear filled her belly, but she kept moving forward.

Nichelle was feeling good that her first encounter with Frank was to invite her to attend worship service with him, this allowed her to open-up and trust a little bit.

She stepped out of the shower and began dressing. Not sure what to wear, she grabbed a simple wrap around dress, a pastel blue, with shoes to match.

She pulled her hair into a bun simple and quick for she was running late, finished up her makeup and topped off the look with a blue necklace and earrings to match.

Just as she did some finishing touches on her makeup, she heard a car pull up into the driveway. She looked at herself in the mirror and smiled but felt off, she decided to change her earrings. Reaching in her jewelry box she pulled out her pearl earrings and put them on. Nodding in approval at them.

"Much better."

Frank arrived pulling up in her driveway, not wanting her to walk too far, his anticipation to see her was getting to him. He felt like he was going to jump out of his skin.

Frank started praying for focus as he's done so many times before.

"God help me to maintain my place as your man of valor, and integrity, and not shame you with my desires for your woman of God." He prayed silently while sitting in his car.

She threw him off balance, taking him somewhere he knew he shouldn't be in his thoughts. But she was just absolutely stunning every time he laid his eyes on her.

He stepped out of a beautiful hunter green Jeep Wrangler, and walked around the other side as she came down to greet him.

She took a glance at him with admiration of how handsome he was and sighed under her breath. As Nichelle reached the vehicle's passenger door, Frank met her there to open it for her, and reached out to grab her hand, feeling the warmth of it making his fingers tingle. He shuddered from within, as he continued to assist her up into the vehicle. As Frank closed the door, he shook his head at how stunningly beautiful and sexy she looked. He rubbed his hand thinking about how soft her palm was to the touch, wondering would the rest of her feel that way.

"God help me." He muttered, returning to the other side.

Reaching the driver's side as he entered, Nichelle tried not to stare, but she couldn't help it. She gazed at his arms as they reached for the steering wheel, how muscular they were, and oh my god, how he smelled so good. She found herself wanting to bury her face in his neck and chest but just shook her head.

"Are you okay, Nichelle?" Franks asked her suddenly.

"I'm fine." she said, as he pulled away from her house.

Chapter 5

They began talking, becoming engrossed in conversation. Nichelle wasn't paying much attention to the turns and stops that Frank was making to get to the building. Unbeknownst to her, his church was also hers.

They finally arrived at the building and as he pulled into a spot, Nichelle looked up to see Mark Jr. her son's car, and realized she was at her church. She chuckled to herself and turned to Frank with wide eyes.

"Frank, this is my church!"

He looked at her, but with a raised brow. They glanced quietly at each other, then burst out laughing.

They laughed so hard and loud that fellow church members pulling in and standing in the parking lot looked over to the car with confused looks.

From that day on Nichelle felt comfortable to spend time with Frank, and attend future events and services with him.

Daily their friendship became a relationship. It moved exceedingly fast, faster than she wanted it to, so she decided to move forward blindly, trusting and eventually falling in love, but not without some reservations.

Nichelle began to realize how fast they were going, just like with Roger. Her blind trust and falling in love had led her to despair, and it frightened her. She tried to open herself again, but one thing stood before her, and it caused her to hesitate and think more clearly.

Nichelle's love and respect for her children and most of all God, made her want to slow down. She'd made a promise to herself and to her kids, that she would not make hasty decisions without thinking of them first. She didn't want to disappoint her babies, God and herself again, because her flesh was weak, because she desired a love of her own here on earth.

Nichelle needed to think rationally, so she went over it again and again in her head saying, "is this relationship conducive to my children and my way of life? what am I doing? This has to stop."

She spoke to herself constantly and began to panic. She felt she needed to end their friendship before she got hurt. So she'd finally decided to meet with Frank and end whatever this was. This would be the day she let go of the very thing she thought she wanted.

***

Nichelle's thoughts finally brought her back to the present, as she arrived at her destination, pulling up to the restaurant and ready to meet with Frank. Ready and prepared to let him go. To let him know this relationship could not continue. This thing they were doing had to stop, it had to come to an end before she lost herself to him.

She had feelings, deep rooted feelings for Frank. Her heart beat so fast every time they were together, she thought about him every day of every minute, and she knew she loved him.

Nichelle knew she could get lost in him, in his eyes, his arms, and his love, but she was too scared. She felt she needed to let him go for her sanity and the well-being and protection of her children.

She was frightened that he would be just like him.

Roger. That he would show his true colors eventually.

She also had not told him about her children. Nichelle

felt once he knew, he would retreat just as Roger did, or

something worse.

Nichelle had no idea that Frank knew about her kids,

and he loved them as he loved her, from the moment he

laid eyes on her.

Frank was sitting waiting for Nichelle, thinking to

himself and pondering how he would propose? What he

would say? How he would say it? Buying the ring and

giving it to her was the easy part. But sharing his

feelings, telling her he knew she would be his, frightened

him.

Frank was nervous and he wanted everything to go

well, but he had an uneasy feeling in his belly, but he

shook it off. He thought to himself, would she cry from happiness? Or run out the room scared? He didn't know much about her, only that he loved the very essence of her. She wooed him, captured his heart in a way he could not explain. He was so nervous; he patted his forehead with his napkin. Frank was sweating profusely and placed it back onto his lap as he waited patiently for his love.

He knew the day they met, she would be his wife, he knew he would spend the rest of his life with her, she was his one.

Frank's thoughts went back to the very first day they met, when he watched her as she spoke about their client. He'd basically hung on every word that came from her mouth; her lips intrigued him. He'd thought to himself, was there a kiss there for him in the corners of her mouth? He was captured by her very presence and still felt the same this very day.

Frank continued to sit patiently waiting, for his soon to be fiancé to arrive, or so he thought. He had no idea what she had in store for him. He didn't have any clue that she was meeting him for the very last time. He was oblivious to her true feelings, and knew nothing of her past, because she chose not to share that with him yet, but he was ready for whatever was to come.

Chapter 6

Nichelle was sitting in her car looking in her overhead mirror, patting her face with a powder puff. She grabbed her lip gloss to put on but changed her mind. She felt this was all wrong and needed to fix it.

Nichelle exited her vehicle and began to walk to the building. Opening the doors, she walked to where she knew he would be sitting. He was at their usual booth, where they have spent nights talking, laughing and giggling from having too many glasses of wine.

Nichelle fixed her eyes on him. There he was, sitting and waiting patiently, she thought. There were two glasses of water on the table, waiting to be consumed.

The table was elegantly set, black ceramic chop sticks sat in the middle of the table on a black napkin, with a candle yielding a gentle flame. The setting that he felt was just right.

Frank turned at that moment to see Nichelle coming towards him. He stood up, watching as she slowly walked between tables to where he was.

Frank gazed at what she was wearing, those white jeans that fit so tightly to her milk chocolate thighs, a place where he couldn't wait to place his lips at, accentuated her goddess figure he admired so well.

She adorned a yellow blouse that he felt flowed on her body like chocolate on a cake pop. She looked amazing, he thought.

Her golden brown locs pushed back into a bun, smoothly slicked to her perfect head, not a hair stood out of place and he was mesmerized.

Nichelle made it to the table and Frank gently took her hand and kissed it, feeling how soft it was in his hand, just as the first day they met.

In his mind he was thinking, 'I can't wait to slide this ring on her perfect finger and kiss it, kiss her and wait for the day I can devour her beautiful body. Lose myself in her.'

Frank's thoughts toward her were beyond sexual, he wanted to be her everything, her King, her Warrior, her Protector, her Lover and her best Friend. He desired to be her Rock; he couldn't think of anything else.

Frank thought of the day he would dominate her on their marriage bed and every day thereafter, taking her to a place only him, her and God reside. He wanted it to be perfect. He knew he had to keep God before him, in order for it to be successful. He wanted to bring their families together, finally meet her boys and girls. He had been waiting for her to tell him about them, but he would explain to her tonight that he knew, and it would not be an issue because he loved them already.

But Frank began to grow a look of concern on his face, because as Nichelle walked toward him, he noticed she didn't look happy. He was wondering what happened, and why she seemed distracted?

After helping her sit he took a seat across from her. He did not take too long and quickly asked her.

"Is something wrong Nichelle, you look concerned and uneasy."

Nichelle stared at him as if she were about to speak, but she hesitated. Her lips pursed together, trying not to just blurt out what was on her heart and her mind. She waited as a few moments of silence passed by. The waitress brought over two plates of Nichelle's favorite sushi dish from the restaurant.

She prepared to eat by grabbing for the chop sticks. But Frank reached over and touched her hand, which sent a whole bunch of feelings flooding through his body, but he stayed focused and stopped her.

"Nichelle, talk to me. You look frightened and uneasy. Did something happen? Talk to me." Frank said to her gently.

Her lips wanted to say his name, but she pulled her hand away and shoved a tuna roll in her mouth. Frank watched as she chewed, loving every time her lips

moved; it sent a flood of feelings through him.

His thoughts took him to the corners of her mouth

wanting to plant a kiss on them, but he just sat back

with the continued concerned look and perplexed as to

what was happening. He could feel and see something

was not right with her between them.

Frank soon followed suit by quietly eating until she

decided to speak, finally talking through the silence.

Nichelle looked at him steadily.

"Frank, I have four children."

Frank stopped mid-pause for a moment. He sat with

his chopsticks down and looked into her eyes.

"Nichelle did I hear you right? Did you just say you

have four children?"

He wanted to tell her he knew, but he felt there was more she wanted to say, so he hesitated to speak. Nichelle continued by answering his question, thinking he was upset, not realizing he was so happy on the inside.

"Yes, I did Frank, and I want to end this thing between us."

A look of confusion came across Frank's face and he didn't understand what was happening, but before he could say anything, Nichelle went on.

"I must end this before I regret it, before you decide to walk out on us, or me finding that my family and I are not for you, or I was a mistake."

Looking perplexed and feeling a pang of hurt and despair, wanting to speak and tell her what she was thinking and feeling was far from the truth, Frank just sat back and waited for his chance to speak.

But Nichelle kept talking, not allowing him to get a word in.

"I can't go through that again. I'm...I'm sorry Frank." She said, in a trembling voice.

Nichelle grabbed her handbag, wiped her mouth and got up to leave, walking briskly through the restaurant, and out the front door racing to her car.

Chapter 7

As she was walking out Frank followed, he called her name, but she didn't respond. He was thinking to himself in confusion, wondering what happened. 'I thought we were okay.' Frank thought in bafflement. He rushed to catch up to her.

He put his hand in his pocket to feel for the ring, assuring it was still there in the box. He felt relieved and continued his pursuit of her.

Just as Nichelle went to reach for the car door, Frank's hand touches hers and held onto it gently, saying, "please, please Nichelle, don't do this. Please stay and talk with me, let's just talk about it."

At first, Nichelle felt instant fear, like he was going to grab her viciously the way Roger did. But Frank removed his hand from hers softly, letting her know she was safe with him. He felt the fear pouring out from her, it was in her eyes and her presence.

But suddenly, Nichelle for some reason felt a safe and protective warmth come over her. Everything around her grew quiet. It stilled the loudness she was hearing in her head; the confusion and fright all became silent.

Her mind was taken out of the present and she felt her memories going back, like a tidal wave they began to hit her full force, and like in a flash, she was back in the past.

***

"Okay Children, my Princes', I need to talk with you." The boys jumped into Nichelle's lap with joy saying, "yes

Momma!" She grabbed them, squeezing them close while sitting on their bed in the small house. She kissed them on their foreheads and began to tell them the big news.

"Boys, we are moving out of this house and into Roger's home."

"Why Momma? why?"

They both spoke at once, each shooting her questions in confusion.

"Why can't we just stay here in our house? We like it."

Nichelle's emotions staggered a bit, but she continued to talk to her boys.

"He proposed to me." She said steadily.

"What's that momma?" Christopher, the youngest one, asked her.

"He asked me to marry him, to be his wife like I was with your dad. He wants us to be a family, it will be fun boys."

Christopher spoke up solemnly, "Momma this does not sound like a good idea, but if you say so and if it makes you happy, I'm okay with it."

Nichelle felt a pang of anxiety, hearing such wise words from her youngest son, but she decided to move forward and trust. It had been five years since she'd been with a man.

The day of the move Roger showed the boys their new room. It was a large space with their own bathroom, it had three beds, two twins and a full.

"Wow Momma, there is a walk-in closet and there are three beds!" the boys said excitedly.

"Who is sleeping in here with us?"

Nichelle looked at Roger and he looked back at her. She knew deep inside that the bed was for her, but before she could try and explain, Roger spoke up.

"Hey guys, the extra bed is for when you boys have friends over, or for Mom. I go away a lot, maybe she can come and sleep in here with you guys, especially if you get scared for the first couple days."

"Cool!" the boys said in unison.

Nichelle and Roger left the room. She looked at him with disdain and he grabbed her by the hair.

"Get in my room now." He said harshly.

Without hesitation, Nichelle walked to his room and he followed behind, shutting the door and shoving her on his California king bed.

He climbed on top of her and said in a low grunt, "that bed is for you, you know that right?"

Nichelle nodded her head slowly. Deep inside she was crying, knowing she had made a mistake.

"You know I need my sleep and you snore really loud."

Roger explained with nonchalance. He began to tell her how his son would be coming soon, and he was not to be disturbed with cleaning, and that would be her responsibility.

"You okay with that?" Roger pulled her hair as if he wanted to subdue her and intimidate her. Thinking to herself deep inside, Nichelle realized she'd made a horrible mistake. But she loved him and had fallen for him.

Roger waited for her answer and he pulled her hair harder. "Yes! Yes." Nichelle responded with regret.

Although he was somewhat violent, he was head over heels in love with her, at least that is what he'd told her.

"I'm sorry, I know you like when I am rough." Roger said, as if placating her.

Nichelle wanted to remind him why, but she didn't want to make it worse.

After he got his answer, he took her right then and there, making what he called, mad passionate love to her. Not caring that the boys were in the next room.

He took her over and over again, until he fell asleep. She tried to get up, but he grabbed her tightly and said, "please, Princess don't go."

He called her Princess because in his eyes she was only a Princess until they were married, then she would be a Queen, his Queen. She stayed with him rubbing his head, all while regretting her decision to marry him and move

into his place.

Chapter 8

Soon Nichelle fell asleep, and Roger nudged her in her back really hard. She didn't hesitate, she knew what he wanted.

Nichelle got up and put her clothes on. As she walked out, he said, "you snore too loud, I need my sleep."

Roger touched her leg as she left the room.

"Love you babe." He said and fell back to sleep.

Nichelle slowly opened the door to the boys' room; they were already sleeping. She climbed into the third bed and cried silently until she fell asleep.

Time went by and Nichelle regretted her decision with each passing day.

'What should I do?' She thought to herself. 'If I try to leave, he won't let me, he'll make a scene and I don't want to expose the boys to this.'

Nichelle thought in fear.

She began to try and avoid him, falling asleep in the boys room before he came home, until she could find a way out.

One Sunday afternoon, a year after the move in with Roger, he requested to speak with Nichelle. He was sitting in the parlor as she came down the stairs. He bid her to come over to him. It was obvious he'd been drinking and had a glass of brandy in his hand.

Nichelle cringed because she knew when he was drinking, he became either horny or angry. He had the glass in his hand, the bottle sitting almost empty at his feet. He began to speak to her, sounding a bit sluggish.

"Nichelle, I made a mistake, You and the children need to move out and find a place soon."

"Roger..." Nichelle replied to him with uncertainty, "what happened, what did I do? You know we have nowhere to go. I gave up my house to move in with you."

Roger just sat there with no expression, sipping his glass. He gave no response to her questions. She was somewhat relieved but devastated at the same time. Where would they go?

"You have to give me some time."

He said to her then, "well until you find a place, you know what you need to do."

Nichelle felt her heart drop down into her stomach. She knew exactly what that meant, and she felt disgusting, like she was a piece of meat. But even still,

Nichelle nodded and turned to walk back up the stairs, forgetting why she came down in the first place.

Her thoughts completely thrown off; Roger stopped her with his next words.

"Meet me in my room, I'm going to take a shower and I want you there when I'm done."

Nichelle was horrified from the conversation, because she knew what to expect, but did exactly what he told her to. Thinking about her children, and knowing they had nowhere to go.

As she was walking into his room, the boys suddenly opened their door and saw her.

"Momma you coming to bed?" Christopher asked her.

"No not yet sons, I'll be in soon"

"okay momma".

Nichelle pulled their door shut and walked into Roger's room, feeling used. As she came into the room, she was about to close the door, when suddenly Roger came out of the bathroom.

"I beat you here, that will be extra for being late." He said to her with a hard look in his eyes.

Roger had his way with Nichelle, he was rough with her pulling her locs, slapping her buttocks harder than usual, he even bit her between her legs in anger.

He finally finished and fell to the bed, kissing her breast, and soon falling asleep.

Nichelle got up to leave and take a shower. But as she was leaving the room, he spoke to her.

"Come back after the boys go to sleep, don't go to sleep, meet me back here again, I need more."

Roger grabbed her and bit her on the butt. Nichelle cringed and gritted her teeth, thinking to herself, 'what have I've done?'

She knew she had no choice, knowing they needed a place to live until she could find them a new home.

The weeks went by, weeks of her sleeping with him, until one night Nichelle decided to stay in the room with the children until she thought he was resting. Praying he hadn't noticed. She decided to go down to the kitchen to get a drink of water and to call her Sister for help, she wanted to do it quickly before she ran into him.

Nichelle walked down the stairs, she moved very slowly. Getting to the bottom of the steps, she suddenly heard him speak out of the dark.

"Where are you going?" He growled, with his deep West Indian Latino accent.

She jumped and dropped her phone. As Nichelle bent down to pick it up, Roger grabbed it first along with her hand, squeezing it tight and almost cracking it, she winced in pain. He placed the phone in her other hand, holding that one tightly as well, squeezing until she again cried out in pain, this time making a squealing noise.

Roger looked at her with hatred in his eyes. He let go of her hand, watching the breath almost leave her body from the pain. He grabbed the other hand again, but this time Nichelle tried to pull it back, but he caught it anyway, holding tightly and squeezing harder again.

Taking her to her knees, seeing her this way, gave him pleasure. Dominating her, making her feel helpless did something to him.

He released her hand slowly, looking into her eyes and seeing the pain as he sat down on the couch in the parlor, drenched in darkness. He was waiting for her, reeking of brandy, a bottle of Cognac sitting next to him empty.

He bid her to come, but she was frightened and took a step back. Nichelle began to walk up the stairs and said to him shakily, "No Roger...I have work in the morning."

He raised his voice slightly saying, "I know you have work in the morning, come here and talk to me."

"No." Nichelle said more firmly. "I'm not in the mood." She stared at him while rubbing her hand.

Roger looked at her with hate in his eyes. Although it was dark, she could see his eyes lighting up as if glowing. Nichelle thought to herself, 'when did he start hating me? When did he stop loving me, or did he ever love me or even had good intentions toward me?'

She was frightened and afraid of what he may do once she started walking away, but he did nothing. Roger simply grunted as she walked up the stairs, slamming the door behind her.

Chapter 9

After that encounter Nichelle began to avoid his advances for weeks, until one night while she was sleeping, she heard the front door open and close, it was him. He came in late, but that was normal due to some of his caseloads, they were late visits.

As he came up the stairs, she didn't just hear his voice, but that of a woman. They came up the steps and went into his room where he had her all night and very loudly.

Nichelle could hear them clearly; he took the woman for hours. Christopher, her youngest son woke up with agitation.

"Mommy what's that noise? Please make it stop, is that person okay?"

"Yes baby, she is okay." Nichelle reassured him. She covered his ears with her hands and began to sing to him until he fell asleep. This went on for weeks. She wanted to tell him to stop, but she knew it would come with a price and confrontation.

***

Nichelle brought it back in, taking a deep breath. She was drifting from that place, coming back from all that pain and suffering.

"Nichelle, Nichelle..." she could hear her name being called. "Nichelle, Nichelle are you okay? Nichelle?"

Frank was touching her shoulder and she jumped, realizing suddenly where she was. She looked at him while standing next to her car, trying to run from the

one true love God placed in her life. Her mind flashed
back to Roger grabbing her, and she knew it was the
reason she was frightened to go any further with
Frank.

Nichelle had in her mind he would hurt her just as
Roger did, deceiving her after she had given of herself,
he would pull the floor from under her. And she couldn't
risk that again.

"No Frank, no I have to go." she said quickly, trying
to brush him off. But he gently grabbed her hand and
spoke to her.

"I'm not him Nichelle, I'm not him. I don't know
what he did, but I am not him. Give me a moment, let's
talk please, share with me. I promise you I will only
listen."

Nichelle thought to herself, it would only be for a moment. He would only listen, what is his motive? We are around people, what can he do? So reluctantly, she agreed.

They soon returned to the restaurant and he led her back to the booth where they were sitting. Her tears began to flow uncontrollably, she was overwhelmed.

Nichelle began thinking of what she went through with Roger and her husband, and how they treated her. It frightened her to give in to another, to be used, her heart and feelings trampled.

This time when they sat, he was directly next to her. Not touching but handing her tissues that the waiter brought over by his request. They sat for hours.

Nichelle began to play back in her mind to before they moved into Roger's house. She thought about the times they spent together alone at his request.

'Meet me without the children at my place.' He had told her, 'use your key.'

Nichelle shared and told all she went through. And Frank listened tentatively, soaking it all in and finally understanding why she was pulling away. Nichelle's thoughts flashed back to the beginning with Roger.

***

One day she met him at his place to find an oasis like atmosphere, there were candles lit everywhere. There were rose petals all over the floors in the living room, up the stairs to the bedroom, and on the bed. Candles lit in the room and in the bathroom, with rose petals in the shower and the jacuzzi style tub.

After dinner and some wine, he walked her upstairs to the bathroom where the tub was filled with water and roses. He kissed her on her hand, then turned her around and kissed her on her neck, taking in her smell, getting high off of her scent.

He then gently helped her take her clothes off. He placed her clothing on a small stand in the bathroom. Roger took her by her hand and helped her down into the jacuzzi style tub. She sat down feeling the heat from the water, and he knelt down beside the tub. He began scooping and rubbing the water all over her back and her breasts, leaning over and kissing her chest. Taking her nipple into his mouth, she gasped and moaned laying back in the tub rubbing her thighs together.

He then reached his other hand down in the water touching her leg, sliding his fingers down her thigh. Nichelle tried to close her legs but he pushed them open with his hand and slid his fingers between her thighs, touching her there and she gasped again.

He reached her most precious possession, feeling how wet it was, he pushed her lips apart and slid his finger into her, she gasped again and grabbed the side of the tub with one hand and his head with the other.

It was like he knew her body, he was well versed with what would take her there. She felt like she would explode, Roger was rubbing her in that most sensitive place, sending her into a whirlwind of ecstasy.

Nichelle couldn't compose herself, she was moaning and groaning like it hurt and felt so good at the same time. It was a sweet exquisite moan, almost inaudible, but sexy.

It made him want her more. He lifted her out of the tub and turned her around right there. He couldn't wait, he had to have her.

Roger stepped into the tub with her and penetrated her from behind. He rocked with her back and forth, side to side, in and out, grabbing her belly and pulling her into him.

Chapter 10

He created a slow and fast rhythm at the same time, making her cum over and over again. Nichelle almost screamed, but before she could, he stopped methodically.

Roger then grabbed her hand, helping her out of the tub and leading her to the shower. He turned the water on, walking her into the spray and gently kissing her other nipple, taking it into his mouth and softly biting it, causing her to moan again her sweet sound of ecstasy.

He penetrated her with his long thick fingers, touching that sensitive place again and moving his hand to the rhythm of her body. Taking her there again and again. He moved methodically, kneeling down in front of her this time and spreading her legs apart.

Nichelle helped him, completely lost in the moment. She leaned against the wall, trying to hold herself steady.

Roger kissed her thighs all the way up until he reached that spot, the core of her sweetness. He lifted her leg over his shoulder, then gently licked her in that moist place. Nichelle moaned and gasped. She cried out over and over again, as he tasted her. Sucking and licking, devouring her as if he could not get enough.

Nichelle's moans were getting louder again, as if it hurt, but it felt oh so good at the same time. She grabbed his head and moved her body back and forth, rocking as if she wanted him more and more.

Roger indulged her, taking her further and further to that place of complete ecstasy.

Nichelle couldn't help it, she let out a scream that was wrenched from her soul. She panted and whispered in a strained voice.

"I'm coming oh my goodness, I'm coming."

Roger kept going and didn't stop until she screamed once last time, along with a "yes!"

He was relentless, he couldn't get enough. He turned her around without hesitation and slid into her from behind. He began pumping slowly in and out, her hands were on the wall trying to grab onto something, but she just moaned and moaned.

Nichelle slapped the wall moaning and groaning, as Roger grabbed her by the belly and breasts, pulling her into him and kissing her neck, pumping in and out of her.

He began to pump faster and faster as he turned her around, then changed the tempo. Sliding himself in again, this time pumping slowly, Nichelle could feel him swelling inside of her.

She then did something he was not expecting. Nichelle pulled away and swiftly knelt down, taking him fully into her mouth. Roger moaned, this time it was his hand that slammed against the wall.

"Damn." He groaned in pleasure.

She grabbed his butt and pulled him into her, as she moved her mouth back and forth, slowly making love to it. Nichelle rubbed it with her other hand, slowly, until she felt it pulsating in her mouth.

she went faster and faster, her hands both holding and rubbing at the same time until an explosion happened in her mouth. Nichelle didn't waste a drop, she swallowed it all. Roger was looking down at her like he couldn't believe what just happened.

He pulled her up to him as the water was running down their faces, and he kissed her and pulled her to him.

Roger looked Nichelle in the eyes and spoke to her with a penetrating gaze.

"Let's get engaged this time next year, for a couple of months, and then get married."

Nichelle hesitated as he looked into her eyes, she was frightened, and he could tell. But he began to assure her.

"Please, I'm your King and you will be my Queen. We can have a small wedding. I know you don't like extravagant things." Roger rushed on.

Nichelle sensed deep within her that he had a motive, but she wasn't sure what it was. The happiness she felt compelled her to say yes, with the assumption the children would be there.

***

Nichelle's thoughts drifted back to the present once again, sharing the warning signs she received and ignored.

For some reason, Nichelle always felt that Roger had never really taken a liking to her older son, Mark Jr., and Jr. really wasn't fond of him at all. Jr. had made his feelings known when she gave them the news, that they were moving in with him. Christopher also wisely gave his opinion as well.

Shortly after the move, all hell had broken loose within their relationship. He'd swooned her and then killed her from the inside out. Nichelle felt Frank would do the same and her trust level was low.

She spoke to him now in a low, subdued voice.

"Frank, he killed me from the inside out. I gave myself to him from day one and continued to give. So giving of myself is not an option right now. I must be rationale, think rationally for my children and for my sanity, and make good decisions that will not lead to disaster. We have just moved into a good place, I'm finally in a good space spiritually and mentally. My job is going well, and I can't mess this up with letting myself get distracted by my flesh, and a relationship that may go sour. I'm working on my relationship with God, working with the youth, and I am very happy doing that." Nichelle got it all out in one breath.

Deep inside she knew what she was saying wasn't fully true, but Nichelle was scared. She had let go so soon with Roger and gave him too much of her and he had almost destroyed her.

She just didn't have any trust for men.

Chapter 11

Nichelle tried to break it down as best as she could.

"Frank, he was a distraction and I see you as the same right now. I need to finish working on me, find me, learn who I am and where I want to go. I'm not getting any younger."

Frank interrupted Nichelle then, leaning forward as if to whisper in her ear.

"You are a wonderful woman and person. I see God working in your life and I don't want to force myself on you. I just want you to know that I'm not him. I'm Frank Martin, humble servant of God. His servant that's not worthy of you, but I know that you are the woman for me. I will wait until God shows you that I am the one for you."

"Frank," Nichelle put up her hand to stop him, "I'm not sure I will ever see that. My eyes are fixed on God and my children. It was nice going out these few months worshipping together, but I am just not ready. Quite frankly, no pun intended,"

Frank smiled at that but didn't interrupt her.

"I'm scared of you, of what can happen. I'm just not ready." Nichelle finished with resignation.

"Nichelle, I'm willing to wait. You trusted and gave of yourself believing he would hold that in high esteem, and he mistreated you. He tainted your trust and tried to control you. He tried to crush your Confidence in man and attempted to take your life, this was the work of the enemy."

94

Frank continued to speak steadily and calmly.

"You need to know that God loves you more and knows you were weak, vulnerable, and afraid to be alone. You fell prey to your own flesh, because it sounded and felt good. You are not the only one that fell for that. Know that Abba, as you call Him, forgives. It's already forgiven, you must and need to forgive yourself."

Frank stood up, and he rubbed her shoulder before he left the table. He walked away feeling hopeful that he would propose someday, just not this day.

'I will always be here when you are ready.' He thought to himself as he walked away, head held up with all confidence.

***

Nichelle remained seated in the booth feeling the reality, the sting, of Frank's words as well her tears, as they rolled down her cheeks.

She began staring off into nothingness, her thoughts spiraling back and finding herself once again at Roger's place.

***

Nichelle walked up the stairs to her room with the boys, rushing them into it, while feeling him behind her. Roger followed quickly behind and grabbed her arm, trying to lead her into his room.

"No Roger, let go of me." Nichelle said in a shaky voice.

He had a very tight grip on her arm but loosened it when one of the boys called out to her.

"Momma you coming?"

Nichelle put her foot in the opening, forcing herself to back away from the door. But Roger continued to make advances to get her into the room with him. He turned her to him pulling, he slid his hand under the back of her head and grabbed a handful of her hair, holding tight and pulling her close to him while looking into her eyes, with his blood red shot drunken gaze.

Roger tried to kiss her. But Nichelle turned her head and face away, finally pulling herself free. He stepped back, holding his hands in the air with a strange look on his face of anger and dismay.

Nichelle quickly ran into the room closing and locking the door behind her. She stood by the door looking back at her sons, they had finally fell asleep. She placed her ear to the door listening and waiting for him to enter, but he gently knocked whispering her name.

"Nichelle."

She whispered back in agitation.

"No Roger, go away please, leave me alone."

After a short pause, his door slammed shut. Nichelle could hear him grunting in anger and slamming himself on his bed. She felt fear that he would put them out in the street or do something to her and the children.

She was afraid to talk to him or be alone in the house with him. Her thoughts continued to swirl around the worst case scenarios of what could happen.

'I must find a place for us to go.' Nichelle thought in desperation. She soon fell asleep wondering what would come next with that man.

The morning arose and Nichelle knew she needed to go grocery shopping, but she didn't want to buy too much, she felt something was coming and they would need to leave abruptly.   Nichelle approached Roger while he sat

in the parlor.

"Do you think you can take me to the Supermarket?"

She asked him with caution.

Roger didn't hesitate, he responded quickly.

"Sure." With his deep accent that attached to her soul

every time she heard it, also knowing he must feed his

son too. On the ride to the Supermarket, Roger asked

her.

"Did you find a place yet?"

Nichelle replied, "yes, just waiting for it to be ready."

She knew she hadn't found anything yet, but she lied to

him for fear if he knew she had nothing, he would put

them out on the street right then and there for sure.

"When do you think you will be moving?" Roger asked.

"Around the first and second week of the New Year, please give me time, I promise we will be out then."

Nichelle realized that God had his own plan to free her from this situation.

A prayer she prayed was going to be answered, only not in the way she would have liked it to be.

Chapter 12

Nichelle still felt something was coming, her spirit was vexed, and very uneasy, she felt he was going to do something drastic. She knew she needed to prepare herself for the worst.

They began preparing for their visit to her sister's home for the holidays. Nichelle got ready for what she felt would be the worst, she didn't want to be caught off guard. They began packing for the overnight stay, at the same time gathering up and securing things they didn't put in a storage unit, into the garage. She would soon learn and feel his plan.

Nichelle and the children were preparing dinner, it was a couple of days prior to their vacation to her sister's house for the holidays.

Roger suddenly came into the house with another female in tow, and he introduced the woman to her and the children. As if he never proposed, like she was nothing, as if they never had anything together.

Nichelle realized that she'd truly made a mistake and that this man was evil, hateful and harmful to the children and her life. Her heart almost beat out of her chest, as she tried to hold her tears back. She did not want the boys to see her cry.

Later that night Roger did the unspeakable again, bringing the same woman into the house. Giving no thought that the woman he proposed to, along with her children, were in his house in the next room. He and the woman had wild sex for hours.

Nichelle's boys asked again about the noise.

"Mommy I wish that noise would stop, it sounds like someone is being hurt."

This time she did not cover their ears and sing them to sleep. She told them it was a movie and turned on her tablet for them to watch something, and drown out the noise.

Morning came and Nichelle was preparing for their departure to Naomi's for the holiday.

"Okay boys." Nichelle said. "Carlotta will be here very soon, take your things downstairs so we can leave for Auntie's as soon as she arrives."

Carlotta was Naomi's daughter, Nichelle's niece. Nichelle and Carlotta shared a birthday and were extremely close, so it wasn't but a phone call for her to come and pick them up.

"Is Auntie coming with her?" Jr. asked.

"No!" Nichelle shouted from the bathroom while brushing her teeth.

"Momma, where downstairs do I put the bags?"

"At the door." Nichelle responded.

Carlotta arrived in her mother's Jeep to assure all their stuff would fit. The boys heard the car drive up. Carlotta jumped out of the vehicle, hearing the boys screaming, "Charley!" from upstairs, as they ran down the steps.

Roger was sitting in the parlor, he stood up in front of the boys and looked at them. They both stopped in their tracks.

"Sorry Buddy." The boys said with hung heads. They knew how he felt about them running in the house.

Roger walked back into the parlor, picking up his book and sat back down, taking a sip from his brandy glass. His glasses were pushed down as he watched from the window, at Carlotta and the boys about to embrace. His look was of jealousy and disdain. The boys were headed straight for Carlotta, they almost knocked her over, pushing her up against the side of the car.

"My dudes what's up? I miss you guys! You guys are growing up, huh? Chris, I think you grew a couple of inches!" Carlotta exclaimed happily.

Mark Jr laughed and said, "I don't think so."

The boys began to load the car with their pillows and blankets along with everyone's bags. They were packed for an extended, extended stay. Nichelle made sure she packed up the kitchen and put all their things in the garage in boxes, to make it easy for their move.

She made sure the room looked as if no one ever occupied it besides him.

When they were leaving, Roger did not even get up from his seat to say goodbye, she knew this would be their last day in this house, but definitely not the last time seeing Roger.

During their holiday visit with her sister and family, Nichelle's phone rang, and she saw Roger's name. She knew it was not good and felt a pang in her belly. She didn't want to answer, but the pangs got stronger and they were terrible. She knew something bad was going to happen. Nichelle answered the phone reluctantly.

"Nichelle." Roger's voice was crisp.

"Yes, Roger how can I help you?" Nichelle replied.

He didn't even hesitate.

"You need to find someplace else to live, you cannot come back here to stay, but you can come back only to retrieve your things."

"Roger," Nichelle spoke in agitation, "Where will I go with two children? You did not even give me a chance. How could you do this to me, to us?"

She started to talk about the babies, but Nichelle hadn't told anyone, not even the children or her Sis that she was pregnant with child. And not just one, but two babies. They would soon find out once she started showing, she had to tell them sooner than later. But for now, she held her tongue and just listened.

"I'm done with you, you are no use to me, I've gotten everything I needed and wanted from you, now it's time for you to go. Let your family take care of you now. You

107

need to make arrangements to come and get your things soon."

Nichelle wanted to tell him off, but he hung up abruptly. She looked at the phone as if what she was hearing was not real. She called him back and started yelling on the phone to his voice mail, but her Sister walked over and grabbed the phone.

"No more Sis, no more, it's over."

Nichelle just sat in the chair and began to cry. Her Sister stood over her and held her, rubbing her back. She cried uncontrollably, her hand on her belly.

Naomi looked down to see the hand on Nichelle's belly and grabbed her face to look at her. Nichelle nodded in confirmation and Naomi gripped her even closer, while Nichelle cried even more.

"What did I do wrong? I messed up; I made such a mistake."

Chapter 13

Nichelle burst out in tears loudly, but quickly remembered she was still in the restaurant.

Her mind came crashing back to her present day and circumstances. The waitress had been trying to gain her attention the entire time. Finally, she heard her voice.

"Ma'am? Ma'am I'm sorry, but we have to ask you to leave, we're closing. Is there someone we can call? Do you need a ride? Are you okay?"

Nichelle looked up with both hands buried in her face, tears rolling down her cheeks. She wiped her face, trying to regain her composure.

"I'm sorry, I'm sorry I lost track of time, oh my goodness the children!"

Panicking, Nichelle jumped up from the booth and ran out to her car. She started it up and began driving as fast as her put-put car would allow. It was old, but it got her around. She needed to get home to her babes immediately.

Arriving home, Nichelle pressed the button for her garage door and slowly drove the car into the garage, not wanting to wake the children. She looked in the mirror embedded in her visor, and grabbed a tissue from the middle console of the car. She wiped her eyes of any tear residue, as well as the mascara that had run down her face, making her look like a cute raccoon.

She wiped the rest of her face and got out the car, gently closing the door. Nichelle walked up the three stairs leading from the garage to the house door. As she put her key in the lock, the door was flung open. A tall and lanky figure stood in front of her.

Nichelle almost screamed from fright, before realizing it was Mark Jr.

"Jr" Nichelle breathed in relief. But before she could say anymore Mark Jr. cut her off.

"Woman where have you been?"

Nichelle just looked at him with that Mother stare and he immediately apologized.

"I'm sorry Momma, but I was worried. It's late and you've never come home this late without calling, and letting us know where you are."

Mark was frowning with concern as he spoke.

"Mom where have you been? We were waiting to eat dinner, but it took you so long we started without you, and then I put the girls and Christopher to bed."

"I'm sorry Jr, it's okay you ate without me. I ate while I was out, I lost track of time talking with a friend. That will not happen again, I promise."

Nichelle reassured her son, hugging him and thanking him for putting the children to sleep.

"Ohhh so when it's my turn to cook you eat out."

Mark Jr. shook his head in sarcasm.

Nichelle laughed, grateful for the humor.

"Momma, were you with that guy from church?" Christopher suddenly spoke up from the kitchen door.

"Sir, what are you doing up?" Nichelle asked with brows raised.

Both her and Mark were startled by his presence. Nichelle hesitated but still answered him, stumbling over her words.

"Ummmm YES! We were just having a meeting."

"Mom!" Jr. decided to address it.

"Yes, Jr?"

"He's a nice guy we all like him, we know he likes you."

"What?" Nichelle was shocked to hear this.

"No! No! He doesn't, how do you know that? He doesn't even know about you guys. Wait, did he tell you that?"

"No, Momma he didn't. But we've noticed the way he looks at you after service, he always says hello, and makes conversation with us."

Christopher, her youngest son responded.

"Momma he seems nice, I like him too."

114

Jr came out of their bathroom at the top of the stairs, with toothpaste filled in his mouth. He had left momentarily but wanted to rejoin the conversation.

"But he has to earn my trust after that IDIOT Roger character. I'm watching out for my Momma."

Jr gave a perfunctory nod, then headed back into the bathroom.

"Where're the girls, Christopher?" Nichelle asked. "They're in their beds, they fell asleep watching a movie after dinner in the den. Jr put them in their bed and kicked me out as well."

"Okay son, I don't want to discuss this anymore. I'm going to take a shower and join the girls in their room."

Nichelle wanted to end the conversation now.

"Okay Momma, but he's a really nice guy. I like his spirit." Christopher said to her, as she walked up the stairs to her room.

Nichelle headed to her room and grabbed a towel from her linen closet within her bathroom, and turned the water on. She pulled her clothes off and dropped them to the floor, immediately jumping in the shower. As she submerged her head into the water, allowing her locs to get wet, she turned around in a circle allowing ever part of her body to be covered with spray.

Nichelle began to stare off into the water, as her thoughts drifted once again.

Chapter 14

Nichelle could see the memories as if they had only happened yesterday.

There she was, standing in her old apartment back in New York City. She was talking with her sons and her brother Robert, about the move to the mountains of Pennsylvania. Robert seemed to understand, but he decided to go to Georgia, to be with his dad in his early stages of Alzheimer.

Robert explained about his Father and how he wanted to help him transition.

"Sis I am so proud of you making a step to change our atmosphere. We all need this move, especially you. If

Mark doesn't want to go, you go. If it gets hard, I'll come back and help out."

"Thanks bro, I believe you would, but I have faith he will change once we are there." Nichelle was so hopeful.

"Keep the Faith." Robert replied.

Mark Sr was standing across the room among the boxes packed and ready to go. Wondering was this the right or best thing to do. Thinking to himself, 'what does she expect me to do with these children, while she is off in another country?"

Not really understanding the move was best for the boys or caring that she would be fighting for this country for them.

Sr's thoughts were selfish and only about himself. Mark Jr looked frustrated that he would have to leave his friends and meet news ones. He asked Nichelle.

"Momma why are you doing this?"

She explained that she would be serving in Kuwait in support to "Iraqi Freedom" due to the events from the World Trade Center bombing.

Jr and Robert nodded in agreement and Sr pulled Nichelle to the side.

"Do we really need to move to the mountains? How am I supposed to get back and forth to work? This drive is going to be just too much for me!"

"Mark, we need to do this for the boys. They need a different environment, and we need a bigger place. You can carpool with Tristan, he travels back and forth to

Fort Hamilton every day, you can do this. Let's do this. It's the best for us as a family and for the boys."

Nichelle hugged him to assure him everything was going to be okay. But deep down inside, Mark thought and knew this would be a disaster waiting to happen, and of course it turned out to be just that.

Mark maintained his excuse that the move was not a good idea and that raising the boys alone was not a good idea as well, but the time was winding down and moving day had arrived.

The children were excited, the neighborhood kids were sad, but excited to help load the truck, but the movers took care of everything. The kids took pictures, ate pizza and talked about the times they had living and growing up in the projects of New York City. They hugged each other, and the young girls had come too.

One young girl named Ciara, cried over Jr leaving. They hugged each other and she kissed him on the cheek, he kissed her on the forehead.

But Overall the kids enjoyed themselves before the truck and car took off. Nichelle let them know that this was not forever, they were only two hours away and they would come back to visit, and maybe even invite them over to their place to visit for a weekend or two.

Between tears and boohoos, they loaded into the cars and the truck took off first.

Nichelle watched as one specific young lady could not stop touching Jr and Jr could not stop touching her. He was crushed just as much as she was and watching this display crushed Nichelle too. The cars took off and the children followed behind, waving goodbye.

***

Nichelle blinked her eyes, as her thoughts came back from the past. She was in the shower, and the water was running down her face and was cold now. She felt the cold water suddenly like razor sharp needles, and she screamed, trying to turn it off.

Christopher came running and busted into the bathroom breathing hard.

"Momma you okay?!"

"Yes, Chris I'm good. The water turned cold."

"Should I check the boiler?" He asked.

"No, it's good. I stayed too long in the shower. I'm getting out now."

"Okay momma, be careful I'm going back to bed, you scared the shsh... I mean the crap out of me."

Chris said laughing.

"I know, I know, no cursing Momma, I'm sorry." He corrected himself quickly.

"It's well Christopher." Nichelle replied, as she reached out to touch his face. "Goodnight!"

"Goodnight Momma! I love you"

"I love you more Prince."

Nichelle looked down at her finger where her wedding ring left a lifetime mark. Its stain, a reminder of her marriage to Mark Sr and all he put her through, after their move to the Pennsylvania mountains.

She couldn't help it, as her thoughts were pulled into that time. And all the pain she had endured.

Chapter 15

Once Nichelle had left Pennsylvania, she vowed she would never return, but here she was two years later, back again trying to start her life all over, after the divorce with Mark Sr.

The boys were playing High School football, basketball and track, and the girls attending daycare, turning three soon.

She'd jumped back from a horrible relationship, violent in nature, to yield two beauties, but with potential danger ahead. The worst of her problems was if Roger found out about the girls, and that they belonged to him. Naomi, friends and her Pastor tried to convince her to tell him, but she knew it would be a disaster. Nichelle didn't want him involved in her life, or their lives. He was toxic.

She thought about how he just threw them out into the streets with the twins in her belly, never sharing it with him. But it was for the best.

Nichelle turned the shower off and stepped out to see her two little beautiful Princesses.

"Boo momma! We scared you, didn't we?"

"Oh, my goodness yes you scared me!"

Grabbing her chest, Nichelle was smiling on the inside.

"Hi mommy, we missed you and wanted to say goodnight." Said Dina.

"No momma, not really." Dana objected. "We were scared. I thought I saw someone in our room. A man standing in the corner looking at us with strange eyes."

"You had a nightmare, a bad dream." Nichelle tried to assure her.

"No momma, there was someone there, he was really scary." Dana insisted.

"Okay, let's go and look in your room and see if he is still there." Nichelle smiled at her babies.

Her girls were so pretty. One had a silky dark-skinned complexion. Nichelle called her beauty, because her skin was so beautiful. The other little one favored Christopher with medium brown skin. She had a smile that could stop and take down the toughest of men, her mother's smile.

Nichelle put on her bathrobe and she and the girls walked to their room down the hall from Nichelle's. The girls stood behind her while Nichelle pushed the door to their room open. She turned the light on and looked around.

"Nothing here." She said in a comforting voice.

But one thing Nichelle did notice was the girl's bedroom window was wide open.

She walked over to shut the window. Looking out at first, Nichelle thought she saw a shadow when she leaned out the window. But she soon realized there was nothing out there.

Nichelle closed the window and turned around to see her little girls laughing and giggling.

"You two are a hot mess! Did you really see someone?" Nichelle questioned them while chuckling.

"Yes, we did Momma!" The girls replied quickly.

"Then what's with the giggling and laughing? Silly girls!"

Dana pointed her little hand at Nichelle.

"Because Momma your robe is open!"

Nichelle looked down to see her robe was gaping open. She grabbed at it, pulling it closed and realizing it was open when she looked out the window.

"Sheesh." Nichelle muttered to herself, shaking her head. She closed their door and shuffled them back to her room.

"Momma the boys were worried about you, Christopher said this is not like you." Dina repeated what she heard her brother say.

"We're so glad you're home Momma!" Dana chipped in.

"Yes, I'm okay babies, I was just taking a shower and then I was going to come and lay down with you."

Nichelle paused and thought about it.

"But since you say there was a man in your room, then you can lay down with me in the den while watching a movie. Would you like that?"

"Oh yes momma we would love that!"

"Let's go watch a movie then." Nichelle smiled as she felt their excitement.

The girls jumped up and down screaming, "YAY, MOMMY YAY! Movie time!"

"Shush, we don't want to wake the boys." Nichelle warned them.

"Too Late." Christopher said, as he walked into the hallway with a very large bowl of popcorn, this made the girls even more excited.

He took the girls down to the den while Nichelle put her night clothes on. As she came downstairs the girls were jumping up and down on the couch.

Christopher went to sit down, but Jr came running in and sat in his seat, and the wrestling shenanigans began.

"Get out of my seat!" one said to the other, and Nichelle just watched, smiling from the inside out.

She hadn't been this happy in a long time. Spending time with her babes was the world to her, but deep inside she wanted a love, a friend, and lover of her own. One day, she thought!

Nichelle and the children fell asleep on the couches in the den. She soon woke up to shuffle the boys and take girls to their room. But the girls prodded her.

"Mommy can we sleep with you?"

"Of course!" She said to them, as they walked into her room.

The girls immediately found their spots, which always began and ended with them sleeping in mommy's arms.

Nichelle thought to herself as she smiled, remembering how the boys use to sleep with her when they lived with Roger. Only this time, they were not afraid or frightened by the noises coming from the next room. Peace and serenity were all they had now.

But little did Nichelle know, that peace would be disturbed soon by an ominous presence lurking, and waiting to attack.

Chapter 16

"California king bed, and they have to lay right on me." Nichelle shook her head and chuckled.

Each girl was nestled deep within her armpits. Nichelle closed her eyes and within seconds, they were all sleep, and she began to dream.

***

She opened her eyes and found herself laying on Roger's chest. 'This is my safe place.' She thought, as she listened to his heart beat. But the rhythm was off, it did not match hers. Suddenly, she felt his hand moving. He grabbed her locs, taking a handful in his fist. He had a tight grip, she could feel her hair pulling from

132

her head. He pulled her head back, so she was looking up at him. Nichelle's heart began racing with fear, she was panicking. Before she could do anything, he then grabbed her around the neck, squeezing his fingers tight around her throat, crushing her larynx.

She began gasping for air looking up at him with confusion, wondering why this was happening. What is happening? She felt herself fading, a tear rolled down her face. She was slowly losing her breath, her air supply was being cut off and leaving her body slowly.

She was feeling herself dying.

***

Nichelle jumped up grabbing her chest, huffing and puffing, gasping for air with tears and fear.

She looked around and realized that it was just a dream. Breathing heavy with tears running down her

face, she remembered the twins were in bed with her.
She looked down where they were laying, taking up lots
of space.

Nichelle shook her head again with a smirk. But then
she began to look at the girls in fear with tears welling
up in her eyes, still sweating and trying to compose
herself, before the girls woke up and saw her crying.

She eased out from the bed slowly, trying not to
wake them.

Nichelle walked to the bathroom to wash her face,
and did something in there she normally only does by her
bed side. she knelt directly in front of her sink and began
to pray out loud.

"Abba Father, thank you for how it all happened and
turned out, for the experience. For I have learned to
only trust you and not man. Thank you for these two

beautiful little Princesses and Princes. I pray you will help me to raise them, to be better at making decisions in their lives, than I have. Thank you for the healing process. It has been hard, and I am struggling in it, but I trust You Abba. I need Your help, If I'm going to make it. I lean not unto my own understanding, but in all thy ways I will trust You. Thank you, Abba, for everything. I know I am not where I should be, but I am truly working toward it. Thank you, Amen."

Nichelle left the bathroom and gently woke up the girls for daycare. The boys were still asleep. It was their summer vacation, so there was no need to wake them.

She dressed the girls one at a time while they were still sleeping. Loaded each child into their car seats and walked back in to leave the boys a note. Nichelle grabbed a piece of paper, and wrote, 'SANDWICHES IN THE FRIDGE, please take the garbage out and load the dishwasher. See You Later, I have a wine tasting later today. I will call you! Oh, the girls are at daycare, Christopher please pick them up at 3pm, Love Mom!'

As Nichelle opened the garage door, she didn't see a figure turn and walk to the side of the house. But there was something in the air.

She stopped in her tracks suddenly, stepping outside the garage and taking a looking from side to side. She felt uneasy for a moment but brushed it off.

Hopping into the car, Nichelle drove out of the garage and closed the door, just as the figure slid under the door, watching as she pulled away.

As Nichelle drove away from the house, her Bluetooth in the car rang. She answered, but realized she didn't have her phone, so she stopped the car.

She remembered her phone was sitting in her bag, which was also in the house.

"Hello?" she said.

"Hello Nichelle."

She heard a man's voice, it sounded like Frank, but Nichelle wasn't sure. It was distorted due to the phone still being in the house.

She backed up into the driveway, and as she was reversing, a man's figure came from around the side of the house and walked in the opposite direction.

Startled to see this, she hesitated to continue the conversation, but Frank said her name again.

"Good morning Nichelle, are you there? I'm calling for church business."

She finally responded. "Hi Frank, I'm sorry I'm in the car outside of my house, my phone is in the house and I'm talking on the Bluetooth."

"Oh that's okay." Frank replied.

"Frank, what can I do for you?" Nichelle said with distraction.

"Can you attend a Ministers Meeting later tonight?"

"Unfortunately, I'm unable to attend. I have a wine tasting at 6pm and will not return until around 9pm. I'll get a message to Pastor letting her know I am unable to be there."

"Do you have another minute?"

Frank didn't want to let her go yet. But Nichelle was apprehensive.

138

"Yes, I have one minute, but I'm running late for a

meeting and must drop the girls off to daycare."

Frank paused but then asked her to attend a service

with him, hoping to receive a yes.

"I also wanted to ask if you'd attend a service with me

this Sunday, in New York City."

"Frank, I can't. I made plans to attend Pastor's

Ceremony for his Bishop Elect Dedication."

Although Nichelle had reservations about attending,

she'd promised Marie she would.

"Why are you not attending?" she asked him.

Frank hesitated to tell her. Although she knew he had

two boys, she didn't know about his eldest son who was

killed years ago. But he made a quick decision, and told

her he was attending a special church service in New

York city.

"Well," Frank began, I'm going to New York City to attend a two-year memorial for my son, at my old Worship Center. He was killed before I moved to Pennsylvania with my sons."

This stopped Nichelle in her tracks, but not about her decision.

"I'm so sorry about your son Frank, but I still don't think it is a good idea for us to see each other, other than to worship together as brother and sister in Christ."

She was trying to stay focused on her family and not lose herself to loving another that may do her wrong, just like Roger. She didn't want to feel hurt again.

Frank felt a lump in his throat and his heart dropped into his belly, but he would not give up, for he knew deep inside she was his one.

"Okay, well you have a blessed evening, and I will let Pastor; I mean Bishop Elect know you are unable to attend the meeting." Frank ended the call with heaviness.

Chapter 17

Nichelle left the car after the phone call to fetch her phone. As she stepped out the vehicle and went into the house, the same figure walked pass the car and looked inside at the girls, closing the door. But not before first pressing the lock for all the doors and gently closing it. He then walked away down the block and got into his car, driving away.

Nichelle soon returned to find that the doors to her vehicle were all locked, and began to panic, but realized quickly that she had a spare key in the house. She shouted out to the boys, inside the house, urging them to bring her the spare key, not wanting to wake the girls. While she waited the phone rang again, this time it was her Sister Naomi.

"Hey Sis, Hey Sunshine!" Naomi said.

"What's up Sis?" Nichelle was happy to hear from her.

"Hey, I would like to meet you for lunch today, you have time for your Sis?"

"Of course I do, where?"

"Let's meet at our favorite place, 'Clarissa's,' The Kitchen Bruja."

"Yeah!!!!" Nichelle was greatly enthused to spend time with her Sis. "Okay see you at noon! I have to go, I'm dropping the girls to daycare and then I have a meeting for work. I'll see you at noon."

Nichelle ended the call and took the key from Christopher as he handed them to her. She unlocked the door and of course the alarm went off, waking up the girls, and they began to cry. But Nichelle quickly got in and calmed them down before taking off.

She arrived at the school taking each girl out one at a time and rushing to take them into the building, not really paying attention to her surroundings, as a car pulled up beside her.

A man got out and walked into the building before them. It was Roger, but Nichelle didn't see him. He walked in to retrieve some paperwork for his client and then left before being seen.

Nichelle hopped back into her car, but as she turned the key, of course, it would not turn over. The car stalled. She became frustrated and continued to try and start the car, but nothing happened. Suddenly she was startled by a tapping on her window.

She jumped and turned to look up through the glass.

Nichelle saw him then, as she stared in stricken fear. Her heart dropped into her stomach. It was Roger. 'This can't be.' She thought in cold panic.

He continued to tap on the window, and she saw his devious smile, a smile that went through right to her soul and froze her spirit. It scared her, made her feel inadequate and wanting to find a sheet to cover her face.

Nichelle was completely stuck, but he spoke to her calmly.

"Nichelle, open your window. You need help, let me help you, it sounds like your vehicle needs a jump."

She immediately came back to her senses.

"NO! Roger please go away, I called someone to come help me. No thank you Roger, please leave, I am okay!"

He leaned down into the car and looked directly into her eyes, his gaze sending a chill down her spine and fear in her belly.

"I'm sorry Nichelle, don't be afraid. I will not press. I'm not here to hurt you. If you need help, I'm just inside with a client."

Roger turned around and walked away with a grin, a feverish evil grin knowing inside how angry he was at her for not telling him about the twins.

"Did she think I would never find out?" Roger spoke furiously to himself, shaking his head but keeping his composure, his cool, not to show any suspicion that he knew.

"I'll just keep a close on eye my girls and Nichelle, until the right moment."

Roger really did not have a client inside, but because of his connections as a BSC worker, he could perform routine no contact visits with one of his old clients. He knew no one would check or call, because of his credentials, and reputation as BSC worker.

Nichelle watched him as he walked into the girl's daycare, fear slams through her entire body, her mind began to run crazy with her thoughts of him being near her girls.

"Oh, my goodness!" Nichelle panicked and jumped out of her car. It seemed las if she couldn't get to the building fast enough. She ran to open the door but slowed down, so as not to bring attention to herself. She didn't want Roger to see her in the building. Although she was a BSC worker as well, she just needed to be careful, she did not want him to know about the girls.

147

Nichelle formulated a story in her head in case he saw her. She walked over to one of the daycare workers and slowly greeted her.

"Hi Berenice," she said.

"Hi Nichelle, how are you doing? Didn't you just leave the girls?"

Nichelle smiled. "Yes, I did. I forgot I needed to talk with Marie."

Berenice nodded. "Okay, I'll help you find her. By the way, how are the boys?"

Nichelle curtly interrupts her saying, "where is Marie? I really need to talk with her! I apologize, but I am running late"

Berenice held up her hands, "It's okay, she is in her office with a BSC worker."

"Okay, Excuse me Berenice!"

Nichelle abruptly walked away toward Marie's office. But as she was preparing to enter, she saw Roger was in there with her. He was sitting, she saw his face and it sent a huge flood of uncertainty of feelings crashing through her body.

Nichelle felt her hairs standing up on the back of her neck. Thoughts of him roughly taking her sexually, the pulling of her hair, the biting of her skin, leaving huge marks, marks that took a long time to heal. The grabbing of her arm and leaving bruises she'd tried to cover with makeup so no one would see.

She remembered everything, all the hell he put her through daily, even the day he put them on the street after giving up her house to share a life with him supposedly. Mixed feelings overtook her mind, body and soul and her spirit. Nichelle felt a vexing but a soothing calm. She didn't know what to do or what to say, but she had to protect her girls, her princesses from this man.

Chapter 18

Nichelle decided to wait. As Roger walked out, she stepped behind a wall near Marie's office, so as to not be seen by him. Roger walked out and Nichelle stepped into the office, furious and scared with fear welling up inside.

"Hey love!" Marie greeted her cheerfully. "Where did you come from? I thought you left a long time ago?"

Without hesitation, Nichelle got straight to the point.

"Marie, does Roger have a client here at the daycare?"

"Yes, he does! He observes with no interaction. Nichelle, are you okay?"

Again, Nichelle spoke abruptly.

"How long has this been going on?"

"About two months, he's been coming since that day you and Frank dropped the girls off."

"Marie I'm sorry, but I'm taking the girls out, I cannot allow them to be in the same building with that man!"

"Okay Nichelle, you are scaring me. What is going on? You sound and look frightened." Marie had genuine concern on her face now. She placed her hand on Nichelle's shoulder. "Nichelle, you are shaking! Talk to me." She gestured for Nichelle to sit down, but she was too worked up and just stood with all intent to leave, with the girls in tow.

"I just can't let them be here while this man is here!"

"Okay, let's talk."

Marie closed the door behind Nichelle and led her over to a chair to sit down.

"Talk to me Nichelle, right now! What is going on?" This time Nichelle didn't hold back. She quickly spoke out of fright and fear.

"Roger and I were lovers, we were supposed to get married, but he hurt me mentally and physically. I don't trust him."

"Nichelle is that all? I can't believe that is all. Spill it!" Marie senses that he is the twin's father. Not holding back, she came out and asked the question. "Nichelle, is he the girls' father? I'm sensing that is why you are frantic?"

153

Nichelle looked down to her French manicured hands, rubbing them and keeping them from shaking, but she was not doing such a good job.

"Nichelle, I understand, and you don't have to say anything else. He is gone. I will talk to him immediately and let him know he must find another way to observe his client. I love you and those girls. We are church sisters, and this is my Center. I say who stays and who goes. He goes! You and my girls mean too much to me and are way too important to me."

Just as they are talking Marie sees Roger walk by her office, but Nichelle's back is facing the door and window so she doesn't see him, and he doesn't know it's Nichelle. He looks in and Marie motions him to wait. He stops and waits for her to come out.

"I'll be right back," Marie says. She stepped out of the office and confronted Roger. She began talking to him. Nichelle turned around to find him looking directly at her with those eyes, the same look he had when he asked if he could help her. She felt that same feeling of fear ripping through her belly and down her spine.

Roger and Marie exchanged words and in a huff of anger, he walked out of the Center, slamming the outer door behind him.

Roger stood outside the building looking at Nichelle's car, he looked back into the daycare, his breathing was strong and long, taking deep breaths as if he had been running a race. Anger welling up inside more than ever. Roger thought angrily to himself.

'she tried to hide those little girls from me, my flesh and blood, now messing with my livelihood.'

He shook his head no, and said with fury, "It's time!" Roger turned back around, looked back once more into the daycare center, and began walking away to his car. He got in slamming the door as hard as he could in a rage of anger. He started the car and took off, tires screeching. Roger began talking under his breath with his thick English West Indian accent.

"Just you wait and see Nichelle Parker, I got something for you...I got something for you."

Meanwhile, Nichelle looked up at the clock in Marie's office.

"Oh my Goodness!!" She realized that she wasn't just late for her meeting, but that it might be finished.

Nichelle jumped up rushing to leave, but not before looking back at Marie. Marie looked at Nichelle with eyes of assurance, that the girls were safe and she need not worry.

Marie mouthed, "I will change all the codes to the building don't worry."

But deep inside Marie felt fear in her belly. She immediately began to pray under her breath, asking Abba for protection, not just for the girls, but for Nichelle and even herself.

Chapter 19

Nichelle reluctantly left to head to her meeting, but she felt the same sick feeling Marie did, as she walked to her car. As Nichelle reached for her car keys, she felt a tap on her shoulder. She instantly grabbed the hand tapping her and bent it, as if to break bones, thinking it was Roger.

She turned to defend herself, letting her keys hit the floor, but she heard a familiar voice slightly raised to get her attention.

"Nichelle!! It's me, its Frank! Stop, I just came to help you, Marie called me."

Nichelle let go and took a step back, seeing Frank standing there.

Frank stood with his hands up in the air as if to surrender. Nichelle looked at him and burst out in tears, flowing down her face.

"Oh Frank! I am so sorry. Oh, my goodness, oh my god!" She looked at him and he saw her, seeing the fear in her eyes, the tears rolling down as she began crying even more from relief than fear.

"Frank!" Nichelle cried out his name as she fell into his arms, laying her head on his well chiseled muscular chest, crying uncontrollably. She said his name again, this time crying harder and grabbing him tight, holding on and not wanting to let go.

"I'm so scared, I'm so scared, please what do I do?"

As Frank's arms enfolded her into his body, she felt a peace immediately come over her for that moment. She felt safe in the arms of the very man who Abba would place in her life to protect her, who she'd tried to run from. Here he was standing firm and strong, ready to protect her from anything or anyone as hard as he can.

Frank wrapped his arms around her tighter, feeling her whole body shaking, he tried not to bask or enjoy in this moment of her vulnerability. She felt good in his arms and all he wanted was to be her everything.

As he held her tighter, the shaking soon began to stop. Frank's thoughts wondered what had happened to cause her this much fear? But he waited until the right moment to ask, when she was more calm.

"Nichelle," he started off, "Can you tell me what happened?"

But Nichelle just laid her head on Frank's arm, while the moment took her back to her New York City apartment. And the memories flooded her.

***

Nichelle walked over to her door, looking through the peep hole. She saw him, and fear filled within her from the inside out, but knowing he couldn't get in made her feel somewhat safe.

"Ernesto," she said breathlessly, "Go away or I will call the Police! I don't want to call them, please just leave me alone."

Nichelle held her stomach, she felt the babies move, jumping wildly, it made her feel uneasy. As she backed away from the door her babies stopped kicking. She wanted to protect them, keep them safe from him. She was afraid if he knew she'd kept the babies, he would

kill her and them. Ernesto was so unstable! Nichelle
turned to walk back to her bedroom, when the door
busted open and Ernesto rushed in and went straight
for Nichelle, grabbing at her.

Nichelle tried to run, but it was too late. He grabbed
her by her neck.

Ernesto spun her around and slapped Nichelle into the
wall, leading to her bedroom. He grabbed her by the neck
again, squeezing tight.

"Ernesto please don't do this, please!" Nichelle pleaded
with her first husband, while gasping for breath.
Ernesto began to squeeze so tight; she couldn't
breathe. She tried to speak, begging him to stop but he
was squeezing her neck tighter and tighter, until her
larynges constricted her from talking.

Her words came out as whispers, Nichelle was gasping for breath, salivating and foam coming from her mouth, she felt her eyes bulging from the sockets, like they would pop out any minute. She could feel the tears rolling down, stinging the open cuts on her face. She grabbed at his hands around her throat and neck, but she was too weak, and he stood 6 feet tall and weighed 300 lbs. He held Nichelle over her bed, feet dangling from underneath her, arms going limp, pants soaked in her urine. She thought to herself, 'I can't believe this is how I die. Abba help me.' she whispered in her mind.

Ernesto looked into her eyes, seeing the tears run down Nichelle's face, and he released her, tossing her onto her bed. He leaned down over her, smelling and reeking of beer.

"You better not tell anyone, you lucky I don't kill you and that baby." He sneered at her.

Nichelle laid on the bed touching her neck, rubbing it and coughing, trying not to throw up, realizing something was wrong. Her back was hurting, and pain was shooting through her stomach like something was ripping her from the inside out. Nichelle tried to get up and walk to the phone, but fell to the floor unconscious.

When Nichelle opened her eyes, she looked around and realized she was in the hospital laying on a hospital bed. She had a tube down her throat.

The door to the room opened up with Mark Sr and her Sister Naomi walking in. Mark and Naomi were crying as they walked in. They saw Nichelle's eyes open and hand flaring. They briskly walked to her side.

Naomi grabbed Nichelle's hand and Mark grabbed the other to keep her from touching her belly. She tried to sit up and pull the tube from her throat, but Mark and Naomi were holding her hands and telling her to wait.

Mark pressed for the Nurse to come. Nichelle was panicking, she was scared, thinking, 'my babies oh my god, please my babies.'

The Nurse came in as well as a Doctor with a syringe, walking over to Nichelle and sticking the syringe in her IV tube, giving her meds to calm her down.

Nichelle looked in confusion because they were still crying. Mark whispered in her ear.

"Nichelle, you are going to be alright. I am so happy to see you awake. Nichelle, I love you and I am going to take care of you."

Nichelle listened to his words as he said nothing about her and the babies, he just said her. Nichelle began to flail her arms, trying to touch her belly, but she felt herself falling asleep.

***

"Nichelle," Frank said softly, but stern enough for her to hear him. It brought her back to the present moment. Her emotions tangling the past and current times. But Nichelle continued to stare off into that space of horror, knowing that she'd lost her babies due to a toxic love. Nichelle's tears began to flow even more uncontrollably, remembering the promise she'd made to herself. She would not get romantically involved with any man after Ernesto. And she'd broken her promise, trying to trust in love outside of Abba.

Chapter 20

Frank's voice was still trying to bring her back, he said to her gently, "Nichelle, please talk to me. Can you tell me what happened?"

Nichelle looked at Frank with hurt and fear in her eyes. Eyes that have seen things no woman should see, but she was relieved that it was not Roger or even Ernesto tapping her on the shoulder. She was so frightened and scared but felt comforted knowing it was Frank.

She knew it would never be Ernesto because he was dead. He had died a horrible death months after she buried her babies, their babies. She felt relieved that he was gone but with some guilt. But her hurt surpassed that feeling of remorse. She was okay with him being gone, but even more hurt with him taking her babies from her.

As Frank held her close, he felt her shaking. He whispered in her ear.

"I'm here, I'm right here, don't worry I won't let anything happen to you. I won't let go until you tell me to."

In her thoughts, in her heart, Nichelle knew and felt this was true. She felt safety at that moment in his arms. He rubbed her on her back with his soft but strong hand, a deep rub that soothed the shaking in her body, all while wanting to do more. But Frank pulled his thoughts in as much as he could, not wanting to take advantage and ruin whatever chance he might have.

While she hugged him, her tiny hands grasping his arms that engulfed her, he continued to bask in the moment being close to her, smelling her. It was tantalizing, taking him to the moment they met when she walked by him for the first time. Frank was enamored by her, wanting her in every way possible, but he continued to not indulge by taking advantage of the moment. He knew he needed her to trust him beyond his reason, besides wanting her as his wife.

The moment was sending Frank into a whirlwind, but he tried to compose himself and not get aroused. But his resolve did not last for long, he needed to be released from her at that moment. It was building up, and he had to put a stop to it. He hadn't been with a woman in nine years and his reserve was leaving him, little by little. Her touch sent a whirlwind of sexual and sensual feelings through his entire body.

He gently pulled her away from his body and held her up softly. He whispered to her, looking into her eyes.

"what happened Nichelle?"

Staring into his eyes with tears flowing and her nose running, Nichelle blurted it out.

"Roger!!"

Frank looked at her and nodded his head knowingly.

"Say no more."

Without hesitation, he walked Nichelle to her car, took her keys and opened the door. Frank guided her in and shut the door firmly.

All kinds of emotions were running through him, Anger, love and including his sexual desire to please her.

But anger had the lead. He shook the thoughts away and muttered silently to himself.

"Lord if ever I needed you, I need you now, I need you right now."

Frank felt a peace pass over him and he motioned for her to pop the hood of the car. He opened the hood, tinkled with the battery cables and signaled for her to start the car. It started right up.

In his mind he realized and understood that this was a serious situation, for he had seen Roger before waiting outside the daycare that day they dropped the girls, but he never thought anything of it. He didn't know why something about the man bothered him, until today.

Frank had seen him drive down Nichelle's block but never thought about it at that time as well. He felt they were isolated coincidences. He knew what he had to do. He had to protect his interest, her family, his future family. His Military and street extinct stood-up in him immediately.

While Frank was fixing the car, Nichelle began to play the whole scenario in her mind, thinking so hard. She thought of the things she should have done.

'I should have told him to go to hell.'

Nichelle thought to herself. She felt angry that she allowed Roger to get in her head, make her fearful. She sat thinking of all the things she could or should have done.

'I should have opened my door and slammed it into him!'

She was so angry but frightened at the same time, her anger boiled, then her curiosity wondered why

172

he was he there. Of all the daycares it had to be this one where the girls were? It just didn't make sense.

Although he was a BSC worker, it just didn't add up. Nichelle felt a pang in her belly like something was coming. Fear gripped her and overshadowed her, she couldn't get past it.

"Abba what do I do?"

Nichelle prayed out loud.

Did he know about the girls? Has he put two and two together?

"Abba," she prayed "I need your help on this. You said, No Weapon Formed Against Me Shall Prosper. I'm scared. You said You don't give us the spirit of fear, but of Power, Love and a Sound Mind, AMEN! I'm trusting You and You alone."

As Nichelle finished up her prayer she was startled by a tapping on her window. It was Frank. She rolled the window down.

"Start it up." He told her.

Nichelle cranked the vehicle and it turned over. Frank bid her to go home immediately.

"You need to rest your mind and body, bring your heart rate down and relax. I'll see you soon."

She nodded in agreement.

"I'll do just that." Nichelle promised him.
She knew the boys were home and she should be okay.

"Nichelle, tell the boys I will bring the girls home, they need to stay with you. I need to do this one thing and then I'll pick them up. Are you okay with that?"

Frank asked her, searching her face.

With some reluctance she agreed. Nichelle felt that the girls were safe with him.

"Yes I am."

Frank reached into the car and kissed Nichelle on the forehead and said, "God got this!"

Nichelle nods in agreement and then pulls off. Both of them not knowing that Roger was still in the area, watching her and Frank the entire time from his vehicle. He watched as Frank stepped back from her car and watches as she pulled off. Roger took off as well and followed behind her. What Roger didn't know or realize, was that Frank was on to him.

Chapter 21

Nichelle arrived home and she pulled into the driveway. Pressing the garage button, she noticed that Christopher's motorcycle was gone as well as Jr's car. They must have gone out before having to pick up the girls.

Nichelle pulled into the garage not looking behind her, and didn't see Roger slip in. She put the car in park, grabbing her bag and keys to the car and house, and stepped out of the car, walking over to press and close the garage door. As she pressed the button, Roger stepped into view where she could see him, just as she turned to watch the garage door go down.

There he was with those eyes, standing 6' 4" tall looking ominous, standing and staring at her.

Nichelle stared back in shock, gasping and dropping everything in her hands, including the car and house keys. She was stuck in the spot where she stood frightened.

"Roger."

Nichelle spoke in a monotone voice, trying not to appear alarmed, as he stepped closer. She still could not move; she was frozen to the spot she stood.

Nichelle turned her head slowly to look at the door to the house, but realized her keys were on the floor.

"Roger, how did you get in here? I don't remember inviting or letting you in." She tried to talk calmly to him.

"Oh yes, my sweet, you definitely let me in."

Roger responded with a smug look and smile on his face. For a moment, her thoughts went back to the night the girls said they saw a man in their room. When that thought came back to her, she took off running to the door only to be met by his arms and hands wrapping around her body.

Nichelle screamed, but towering over her at 6" 4' tall, Roger put his hand over her mouth, pulling in tightly enough for her to bite him.

Almost breaking her neck, he whipped her around by her head and with the back of his hand, slapped her to the ground. He grabbed her up and pulled her by her hair, pulling her close to him. Wanting her to feel that he was hard and kissed and licked her on her face.

"Oh my, Ms. Nichelle!" Roger sneered with his thick accent. "Your hair is much longer for me to grab and pull!"

He grabbed it and yanked hard.

"Let's go into your new house, I want to see what it looks like!"

Laughing with a devious tone that made her shiver, Nichelle already realized he had been inside her house, around her babies.

This frightened her even more. She now wondered if he did something to the boys. Trying to focus and see, Nichelle felt blood running down from her nose, she was at point of almost passing out. He grabbed her again, standing her on her feet.

"Oh no sweetheart, wake up, I need you awake for this." Roger chuckled in anticipation.

"Roger, please, the children may be home." Nichelle pleaded with him desperately.

"Now you and I both know the boys are not home, both their vehicles are gone, and those precious little girls are at daycare."

He looked at her shaking his head, grasping a handful of her locs and yanking and pulling her further into the house. He Looked around the kitchen, scanning to assure there was no one else in the house.

"Nice kitchen, hmmm bigger than mine, you did good for yourself huh, Queen Princess? I want and need to talk to you Nichelle, you have some explaining to do my sweet."

"I am not your sweet nor your sweetheart, you can go to hell!" Nichelle shouted at him in a fit of fury.

She fell forward clumsily from having exerted what little energy she had.

"Oh, that's okay dear I will, and I will take you with me, but not before sending those little girls to my mother in my country. You will never see them again."

"NO!!!!" Nichelle screamed in panic. "Please, Roger don't take my babies from me!"

"Well we will see about that!"

Roger viciously pulled her by her hair again, dragging her behind him. She could barely walk, feeling dizzy and trying not to pass out from him slapping her.

Why is it that when a man slaps a woman it's like he knows exactly how to hit her, and render her unconscious, or without the ability to fight back?

Nichelle winced in pain; her head was hurting. She could barely see, everything blurry. Her face was feeling

181

tight and it was swelling up, but thankfully she did not pass out. She did everything she could to keep herself awake.

Roger mustered up an apology with his accent (which sounded thicker than ever) for slapping her.

"I'm sorry for slapping you so hard, but you bit me, and it hurt. I can't help it; I'm feeling so much anger toward you right now my sweet. What did I do to you but try to love your hateful ass!"

Nichelle managed to walk without stumbling. Roger walked her toward the den first, looking around and holding her tightly to him.

"Maybe I should have you in here and then upstairs so you can have the memories of me doing you well in every area of this house. Do you still do that thing with that beautiful mouth of yours? You knew your way around a dick, huh girl? I would love to experience that again, but I'll pass my sweet, for I am sure you would love the opportunity to bi... yikes I can't even say it. But That's cool, I'll just beat that pussy up real good."

Roger laughed a deep hardy laugh that just ripped through her whole body. She was scared but was ready for whatever he had for her, she was ready to fight.

Chapter 22

"Roger don't do this; whatever it is you are doing it will not turn out good for you." Nichelle made a last attempt to reach him.

"Oh, my sweet I prepared for whatever happens, as long as I take you with me. So now take me to your room where all that magic happens with Mr. tall dark and handsome."

Nichelle thought of who he was talking about, quickly realizing he was referring to Frank.

"Besides, I just want to talk to you, so take me to your room. NOW!!!"

"Okay, okay up the stairs the first right and then left".

She tried to take him to the attic, but he already knew that it was the attic.

"No, we go right again, that's the attic on the left." Roger grabbed her, pissed off and pulling her to him with his breath directly in her face.

"Don't try to lie to me Nichelle. I know you know I've been in this house before."

Her thoughts swirled of him being in the house with the girls. 'Oh my God.' Nichelle now realized his agenda was real about taking her to hell with him.

She felt sick as she tried not to throw up but does. "Oh, are we pregnant again for Mr. or is it just settling in that you know I've been in this house before? Tsk Tsk Tsk someone has been naughty. I know Mr. has never stepped a foot into this house I just wanted to see if you would tell it. So how do I know this?"

Roger asked her, enjoying the moment.

"Because you've been watching us, you sick coward!" Nichelle snarled at him.

"BOOM my sweet! Now let's go in and get this over with, I have two little girls to meet."

"Roger please, let's talk civil. I want to talk, I'm ready to talk."

"Oh, we will talk after I have satisfied my appetite with that delicious body of yours. I remember how sweet it was, yielding to me every time. I have never met, found or had a woman as delectable as you."

"Oh really?" Nichelle snorted sarcastically. "I couldn't have been that pleasing, that it was so easy for you to throw me away like a piece of garbage?"

"Dear Queen, you were definitely not garbage. Garbage don't taste that good, no matter how much you clean it up. You my dear, are sweet as a cherry pie. You just had and still have way too much fight in you. I knew it would be hard to tame you. I didn't have the time nor the energy to break you, and it seems like you still need breaking. So, let's get started!"

They moved toward her room.

"Please, Roger! Please don't do this."

Nichelle tried to keep him from taking her into her room. Roger raised his voice in impatience.

"SHUT UP! I'm in control and I have the floor." Trembling, knowing that was was going violate her, Nichelle tried to think of something. He smelled, reeking of Brandy, as he led her into the room.

"Wow a room fit for a Queen! I love the décor, this is all that was in your storage container. I should have had you bring it to my place and then sold it, I could have gotten a pretty penny for it, especially that mirror."

Roger took a moment and stared in envy.

He took the lamp from the dresser and slammed it into the mirror, shattering it into pieces. Nichelle held her head down, ready to cry for the only gift Mark gave her that meant anything to her, besides their boys.

She felt like the night Ernesto took her babies from her, helpless and vulnerable. 'Why does this man hate me so?' she thought to herself, feeling numb.

As they walked further into the room, Nichelle protested, pulling in the opposite direction. Roger yanked her into the room. He saw the pictures of the girls and he slammed her down on the floor, in front of where the pictures sat, and put his foot in her belly, slamming it down and rendering her unable to move.

Nichelle coughed roughly, blood coming from her mouth. She tried to curl up, but his foot was directly in the middle of her belly. Unable to move, she laid on her back praying this would end quickly.

"Now who are these pretty little girls? They do look like you, but they also resemble someone I know all too well. One dark and light like you and I. Your light skin and my dark skin, you did good Nichelle."

Roger remarked in observation.

Nichelle didn't speak. Roger bent down over her and got close to her ear, whispering with anger in his voice.

"Nichelle, WHO ARE THEY?"

"They are my daughters." Nichelle replied weakly, wincing in pain from his foot in her belly. His voice vibrated right through her, and she was frightened from the inside out.

"No Nichelle! They are our daughters, my daughters. I know about them. I've known about them for quite some time now. I have been waiting patiently for you to tell me about them. Why haven't you told me? I have rights as their father."

"I haven't told you because they are not your daughters, that's why!" She shot back at him.

Roger moved his foot from her stomach to take a picture out of his pocket. As he did, Nichelle pulled herself up trying to get away, but he kicked her in her stomach, causing her to move back to the spot where he threw her down.

He pulled the picture and held it up next to the girls' picture, and then shoved it in her face.

"Who is this Nichelle?" He demanded. "speak up, I cannot hear you!"

"It's Jacqueline your daughter."

"That's right and she looks just like these pretty little girls. They are so sweet, they sound sweet. They shared a lot of information with me at the center, right before you ruined my visitation rights to my clients."

A look of horror came over Nichelle's face and she began to throw up again.

"You sure you're not pregnant dear? You seem to keep doing that!"

"I hate you Roger!"

"Yeah, a lot of people hate me, but they will get over it, and so will you."

"The girls are not yours; they are the man you've seen me with. He and I have been dating for a long while, directly after you threw me to the curb, so the girls are not yours." Nichelle tried to convince him.

"Why do you keep harping on that? Get over it. No! They are mine, I have been watching you for quite a while. When you moved into that battered women's shelter, I found you there. I watched you on several occasions as you waddled from the car to the building, you looked so cute, but I could just strangle you hiding my babies from me. You denied me the opportunity to see them come into the world. No, you don't lie very well Nichelle. You can't lie! Even when I was giving it to you good, fucking the shit out of you, before you decided to not share the sweetness of that delicious pussy of yours anymore. You would try to resist me, but you gave in every time, moaning, calling out my name and clawing me,

giving it to me. That's why I enjoyed you so much. You

yielding to me, satisfied my appetite."

Roger smirked at the memory.

   "So, because you lied to me, I'm going to make you

pay for it real good. I'll plant another seed, so I have

the pleasure of witnessing my child be born, you robbed

me of that."

   "I will never have another child for you." Nichelle said

with disdain.

   Roger slapped her hard again and this time she fell

forward, hitting her face on the corner of bed.

Chapter 23

Nichelle fell to the floor, dizzy and unable to see due to the blood rushing from her face into her eye. Blood was getting everywhere. Roger saw a towel on the floor near the bathroom door and he grabbed it, wiping the blood from her face and hands it to her, telling her to hold it tight. Nichelle could barely sit up let alone hold a towel to her head.

He decided to take her anyway, blood and all. Roger grabbed her off the floor and threw her onto the bed. Nichelle tried to speak and said with a rasping voice.

"Roger... please stop."

She started to remember what Ernesto did to her. How he choked her until she couldn't see and slapped her up against a wall busting her face open. A flood of memories came to her, she began to remember her childhood. She remembered all the men that had taken from her, deposited their toxins in her, leaving her empty for many years to come.

She remembered what her Uncles and Cousins did to her as a little girl. Holding her down, taking turns raping her and performing sexual acts with her. Taking her virginity, using her little body as their playground.

'Abba!'

Nichelle screamed it in her head.

'please don't let this happen to me again, please!'

As she laid once again helpless, with no one to rescue her from once again being ravaged, abused and misused.

195

She continued to Plead with Roger to not do this lude act to her.

Roger pulled her pants down while she tried to muster up a scream.

Nichelle kicked her legs, but her head was hurting so bad she had no energy whatsoever. She was dizzy but she continued to struggle and fight, flaring her legs and kicking him between his legs, wounding him.

Roger dropped to the floor yelling out in pain. "BITCH!"

But he got right back up. Nichelle tried her best to get up and fight some more, but she still had no energy. She continued to call out to Abba, her Father. 'please help me!'

Roger came back for more, excited by her attempts to fight him, wanting to cover her mouth, but he remembered she bit him the last time. So instead he grabbed her by the throat and squeezed, choking her until she passed out. When she went limp, he pulled his penis out and proceeded to penetrate her. Spreading her legs with his legs and climbing on top of her.

Nichelle took a breath, slowly coughing and trying to sit up and he pushed her back down with one hand, while the other was holding his penis. He was anxious, wanting her, knowing her body would yield to him and take him to ecstasy, that place that only resided within his head.

Just as he was about to penetrate her, Nichelle opened her eyes, her vision was blurry, but she saw a large figure come through the door standing behind Roger.

The figure quietly grabbed the lamp Roger used to smash Nichelle's favorite mirror with. He slammed it over Roger's head, causing him to fall to the floor. After which he began to punch Roger over and over and over again until his body goes limp, dropping him to floor when he exhausted himself, and Roger was no longer moving.

Nichelle laid listless on the bed with blood and tears streaming from her face, trying to get up, but she flopped back down as pain ripped through her body. But she felt relieved seeing Roger laid on the floor, not moving.

She finally saw the face of the person that saved her. It was Frank.

Nichelle reached out to him and tried to say his name, but has no voice and was exhausted from the fight and being hurt. She was in so much pain, and just began to cry. But her tears were of joy and in her mind, she said softly, 'thank you Abba, thank you for saving me.'

Frank walked over to the bed to assist Nichelle with pulling her pants up, but she was weak, so he did it for her gently. He then grabbed a blanket to cover her and ran to the bathroom for a clean towel, to put on her face to stop the bleeding. He retrieved one from the open linen closet. He wiped her face and pressed the towel to her wound, a large gash in her face from hitting the side of the bed, Nichelle felt a relief in her spirit.

Frank assisted Nichelle up from the bed.

"Can you walk? I will help you, lets go slow."

Looking down Nichelle saw Roger laid out on the floor. She turned her face, not knowing what happened to him and she didn't really care. She just wanted him out of her house.

"I'm gonna go downstairs, the Police should be coming up soon." Frank said to her.

Just as he left her to walk down the stairs, the Police came along to assist her. She stopped Frank, gesturing with her hands.

"Don't do nothing crazy, let the Police handle him, please Frank."

Nichelle said to him, just as she fell into the arms of one of his Police officer friends.

"I got her Bruh!" she heard, just before she passed out.

"Nichelle, Nichelle..."

she heard her name very faint, but it faded away.

Chapter 24

Nichelle opened her eyes almost jumping out of her skin, almost screaming but unable to, as she had no voice or the energy to do so. Her arms were reaching, pushing and fighting.

Frank and Naomi came to her side, this time not holding her hands or arms to keep her from touching her belly, but to calm her down and let her know she was okay and safe.

She called for the girls and her boys.

"Dina, Dana, I need to see them please. Where are my babies?"

Nichelle was frantic to see her kids.

"Where are Christopher and Mark?"

Just as soon as she finished saying Mark's name, the children came walking into the room. The girls saw her and yelled out.

"Momma!!!" they shouted in unison. "Momma what happen to your face?"

Dina and Dana said looking at her. Nichelle realized she was only seeing out of one eye, and she tried to get up from the bed, but both Frank and the boys stopped her

"Nichelle!"

"Momma! Where are you going? You need to rest."

"No, I want to see my face, let me up, help me. I don't remember much after Roger hit me. How does my face look? Please somebody get me a mirror, please!"

Nichelle was crying, starting to panic.

Naomi walked over to Nichelle.

"First let me tell you that your face will heal, and the surgeon did a wonderful job, she happened to be a plastic surgeon knowing your H.E.R.S.T.O.R.Y. she fixed you up good. Your left eye, nose and face are swollen, but...."

Naomi paused and Nichelle was frantic.

"BUT Naomi!! What?"

Naomi was hesitant to speak, so Frank walked over and whispered in her ear.

"Nichelle, I am not like the others, what I say is what I mean. I love you, every part of you!"

Frank grabbed the mirror in Naomi's hand and gave it to Nichelle. She took it in her hands and slowly lifted it to her face, while everyone in the room watched and waiting for her reaction, after looking in the mirror. It was so quiet she thought it must be really bad as Nichelle looked at her family's faces, her sons Mark and

Christopher, her baby girls Dana and Dina.

Her sister Naomi, and lastly Frank, her present and

future love forever. She decided not to look. Nichelle put

the mirror down and held her head down and then up.

In that moment she was taken back to the day she

gave birth to the girls, one of the best days of her life,

just her and Naomi.

Nichelle remembered the day Naomi picked her up

from the shelter and they went for a ride and had

breakfast at their favorite restaurant Clarissa's.

She thought back to that day when they left. There

was someone sitting in a car parked against the wall

across from the center. She thought back to what

Roger said about seeing her at the shelter. Roger was

there that day. It was him parked up against the wall

across from the shelter, he had been stalking her.

204

Nichelle remembered after they sat and talked for

hours laughing at the restaurant.

When they returned the same car was still parked on

the wall, a man sitting in it. He had a book over his face.

She remembered because Naomi asked if he was

security. Nichelle shrugged it off, but what he'd said

stayed in her head now, as she realized it was him

watching her.

As they'd gotten out of the vehicle, Nichelle's water

broke and Naomi rushed to get her to the hospital.

The car moved when they moved, he'd followed them

to the hospital close enough so he wouldn't lose them.

Naomi dropped Nichelle to the front of the hospital

for her to be taken to the Labor and Delivery

department, while she parked the car. He was there in

the building; she saw him as she was wheeled into the

elevator. He'd waited for the next elevator his head was down, but she now realized that she'd recognized the face of her baby's father.

While thinking about this amazing event in her life, not once did she feel fear anymore, but she felt disgust of this man who'd tried to ruin her life.

Nichelle remembered being scared she wouldn't have the girls naturally. She'd worried she would have a cesarean, and she didn't want to be cut open. At her age it was already risky being pregnant, then to be having twins another risk, but Naomi was there to help her and guide her through.

Nichelle remembered she labored for hours, 14 to be exact, until Dana came down the canal first. She was somewhat in distress, but she was able to push her out.

She pushed three, times Nichelle remembered, and there came Dana screaming so loud. Then Dina came.

Nichelle was relieved there was no cesarean and the girls were healthy. Only thing wrong during and after birth was Nichelle's blood pressure was a little out of whack and she needed to stay an extra couple of days to assure she was not going to stroke out. The day they left the hospital, there he was again in the lobby in the corner with a fitted baseball cap, that covered his face as he looked down the whole time.

Nichelle remembered because someone called his name, they thought he was someone else, at least that's how he made them feel, but Nichelle recalled the name and the sentence.

"Hey, Roger how you doing?"

But he'd just ignored the person and they just walked away. It was all coming back to her, that this man was stalking her the whole time, even after he put them out on the street with nowhere to go.

"Nichelle," Naomi said, "Nichelle!" She jumped, coming back to the present.

"Are you okay?"

"Yes I am. I am now, as long as I never have to see him again."

Nichelle began to cry, and Naomi leaned over the hospital bed and held her, but Nichelle was too overwhelmed.

The Nurse walked in soon after to administer a sedative.

"Ms. Turner I have something to settle you. Your heart rate is a little high and that's normal with what you've been through. The Doctor would like you to relax and bring your blood pressure and heart rate down."

Naomi took this as her que to leave and allow Nichelle to rest, but not before letting her know the girls would go home with her.

"Sis my nieces are safe with me, don't you worry."
"Thank you, my love, my Queen Sis, you are amazing."
Nichelle was grateful for her sister.

"Don't think I forgot about that fiasco with my brother in law, I'm coming for him."

Naomi chuckled but knew the situation must be addressed before all hell broke out.

Chapter 25

Frank and the boys walked over to the bed to hug Nichelle, Frank stepped back and let the boys get their hugs in and motions to them, he will be right out.

The boys smiled and laughed slamming into each other on the way out.

"See you later Momma. We love you. Momma, get some rest."

"Yes, I will, boys, I promise." Nichelle assured them.

Frank moved forward wanting to hug her, but not wanting to hurt her. Also, knowing his limitations when it came to physical contact with her. He chose to stand just arms-length from her, and she reached out for his hand and pulled him close.

"Thank you, Frank, for being there for me. Maybe, just maybe I'll give you a chance. Be patient with me."

As he basked over the closeness between Nichelle and himself, he talked silently to Abba.

'thank you, Abba, I will wait.'

Nichelle looked at Frank and kissed him with a kiss he had been waiting for, he had been eyeing the side of her mouth, longing for it since the day he laid eyes on her. It was just as he dreamed it would be and more, he would love her forever.

"Take care of my boys for me, I'll see you in a couple of days, we have dates to make up for." Nichelle said softly.

Frank Smiled while continuing to bask in her arms, the glorious touch of her arms wrapped around him, how soft she was, everything he imagined. She felt just as he imagined and touching her hand made every sensual, sexual manlike feeling radiate through his body. But he made a silent and fervent vow to himself.

'I must hold out for the day she becomes my wife, and then, we can write a new S.T.O.R.Y.'

***

Meanwhile, at a Pennsylvania Federal Prison, sat Roger, mulling over his wounds he received from Frank, and thinking how he could get back at Nichelle.

'I know I have rights as a father.' he thought to himself. As he sat there, some inmates were eyeing him from across the room.

Roger realized that he had gotten himself in a bind and was not really sure how he was going to get out.

'But my time will come soon.' He thinks with insane rage.

As he walked over to the inmates immediately, he speaks to them briskly.

"I have a proposition, and a lot of money to offer!" One of the inmates smirks.

"Oh really, you do now? Well bruh, listen Mr. suit, because you look like you a suit, like you from wall street or something. So, let me school you chump. I know about you; I know you beat women. We don't like that shit in here and we feel the need to show you how to treat a woman, a Queen. I hope you know who I am talking about."

Roger had a look of confusion like, what is he talking about?

213

"Yeah, you don't know what or who I am talking about, do you? Does the Name Nicky, ring a bell? Oh, wait only I call her Nicky! Nichelle!"

The inmate said the name, and fear rips through Roger's belly, for he knew he was in trouble. As he and the inmate stood up, one he didn't know the name of, along with several other inmates standing with him, Roger realized this would be a battle for his life.

The inmate got really close to Roger's face and said to him.

"Dude, my name is Charles, and this is my crew and Nicky is MY Sister, you feel me?......"

Just you wait and see what happens next......

Epilogue

Little girls should never see the things I've seen as an adult, for this adult as a little girl has seen and experienced it all, listen closely. As a little girl my cousins, my Uncles and family friends have touched me, raped and violated my body in ways that would make the strongest man weak in the knees and sick to his stomach.

This book speaks about what I went through as an adult woman who attracted all the wrong men in her life. Men who had no care or respect for me as a young woman, mother, sister, daughter and Queen. They ruined me from the inside out took away my self-esteem, as a child and as an adult. Made me question everything good bad or indifferent in my life. Not that we shouldn't have questions, but the kind that went through my mind and thoughts.

I trusted no one, not my mother, my father, my sister, my brothers, my cousins, my aunts, my uncles, and even my husbands, because they all played a part in what was done to me in my eyes. The cycle continued on and on until I decided that it would not. I gave birth to five daughters and two sons. I asked God to please not let what I experienced in my life happen to my baby girls, my princesses. Well it hit home for two of my daughters, and it just destroyed me even more on the inside.

215

I became overprotective, tried to and wanted to keep them close. I did not allow anyone close, I did not allow anyone near except for a few friends and some family. But come to find out they were using me too, why I do not know. So, I eventually had to let them go as friends and even kept family members at bay. Not that I didn't love them, I just didn't trust.

No woman, man, little girl, or little boy should experience that type of life. A life where you are suspicious of any and everybody you meet. No child or adult should have this same story, a story so sickening and unspeakable. It saddens me to know that there are many, a myriad of children, women and even men who know my story all too well.

My prayer is this book, my book, and my story opens the eyes of mothers, and fathers all over the world to the signs of their little girls or little boys, and teenage girls, teenage boys who are being abused mentally, sexually and physically right under their nose. I hope and pray deeply this book sets any woman, man, boy or girl free, from this cycle of abuse.

I have endured this for many years and after telling my story, putting it on paper, I am liberated, I am free from this abuse. This cycle will be and is cut from this blood line. I declare that anyone I know that is close to me who is enduring abuse mentally, physically and

216

sexually will be liberated just as I have and will seek help in their lives to be healed.

As you read this book, part 1 of a three book series to my story, know that it will lead to healing, complete healing in your mind, your body and soul only if you are open to it.

Thank you for reading and sharing in the beginning, middle and complete stages to my healing.
May Abba bless you immensely.

- CarlottaAne'th

About The Author

I am a mother of seven, five Beautiful Queens and two handsome Young Princes. I'm a grandmother who is head over heels in love with her grands, two Princesses, and three Young Princes. My favorite places are to spend at my middle daughter's and oldest daughter's home where I get lost in time hanging with my babes. I love my book area where I also get lost in time reading and writing. I love music, reading, dancing and being absolutely silly with my family. I love being in love with ABBA, myself, my children and that special someone. Family is Everything as you have read. Currently residing in Northeastern PA, grew up in Flushing Queens, NYC, but adventure is calling my name... Movement is inevitable! With Movement Comes Change and with Change Comes Movement!

CarlottaAne'th is also a radio host personality on Jewell's Diamond in The Rough Podcast, as well as a veteran in the U.S. military. To learn more about CarlottaAne'th and her upcoming books of love and inspiration, visit the publishing website at: www.AJBPublishing.com

www.ingramcontent.com/pod-product-compliance
Lightning Source LLC
Chambersburg PA
CBHW030543030726
47495CB00004B/1104